A Return to the Alamo

British Army deserter Thomas Collins is working with the Texas Rangers in Galveston to secure a supply of gunpowder, which is desperately needed back in San Antonio for the continuing struggle against the fearsome Comanche Nation. Unfortunately, Thomas's past catches up with him in the form of a ruthless British army officer, Captain Speirs, who has been sent across the Atlantic to apprehend him.

As Collins and the Texan Lawmen slowly drive their heavily laden wagons back to San Antonio, they are relentlessly hunted by Speirs and his men, attacked by the forces of a powerful former president of the republic who wants the gunpowder for himself, and harried by a Comanche war party. Thomas has to take command of the Rangers to ensure they reach San Antonio safely, but faces some tough decisions when his lover Sarah is kidnapped by Speirs.

A Return to the Alamo

Paul Bedford

A Black Horse Western

ROBERT HALE

ISBN 978-0-7198-2063-2

The Crowood Press
The Stable Block
Crowood Lane
Ramsbury
Marlborough
Wiltshire SN8 2HR

www.crowood.com

Robert Hale is an imprint
of The Crowood Press

*For my lovely wife Susan, who hasn't actually
read any of my books, but I can live in hope*

Typeset by
Derek Doyle & Associates, Shaw Heath
Printed and bound in Great Britain by
CPI Group (UK) Ltd, Croydon, CR0 4YY

CHAPTER ONE

Myriad lights all along the shoreline heralded the arrival of dusk. The city of Galveston lay before us in all of its sparkling glory. From where we hailed, such unguarded excess would be a sure way to hear God laugh. Nobody living in West Texas in the Year of our Lord 1845 would dare to offer such a tempting display. Distance from the settlement line, added to the safety of living on an island, had obviously created a completely different mindset in the inhabitants of the Republic's erstwhile capital city.

Idly leaning against a guardrail, I listened to the water lapping against the timbers. The absence of grinding toil on my part, coupled with the gentle swaying of the ferry was almost sufficient to lull me into a false sense of security. As the cumbersome craft's burly operators heaved on the thick cable, I glanced around at my companions. The seven grim faced rangers showed no sign of relaxing their vigilance. Brutalized by the harsh realities of frontier life, they were men with few illusions. Their hands never strayed far from their weapons and any conversation was curt and controlled. Catching my eye, one of their number drifted over to my side.

At first glance, Ranger Sergeant Kirby was an unlikely looking guardian of law and order. Older than the average pistol fighter, with a swarthy piratical visage, he neverthe-less possessed a level of intelligence that marked him out from his companions. As with all Texas Rangers, he did not wear any recognizable uniform. A buckskin frockcoat worn over a linen shirt extended almost down to his knees. On his head he sported a broad brimmed felt hat. Tilting this back slightly, he eased forward until we were literally almost nose to nose. His rancid breath was very nearly over-whelming, but I resisted the temptation to retreat. At that stage in our journey I did not relish an involuntary ducking.

'It's too late in the day to start prospecting for powder,' he remarked. 'We'll bed down for the night and start fresh in the morning!'

I favoured him with a pained expression. 'How I long for freshly cooked food and a mattress. Do you know of any reputable establishments?'

Kirby stared at me, a faint smile playing on his weath-ered features. 'Galveston's a mite hard on the poke and rangers' pay don't allow for no fancy hotels. Won't be the first time we ended up bedding down next to horseflesh in a town.'

'If you think that I'm going to sleep in a stable like the Virgin Mary, you are sadly mistaken,' I protested. 'I am in funds, as long as you don't mind accepting hospitality from the British government.'

'I'll take hospitality off of anybody that offers it. And if it's high living you're after, Tremont House is the place, but don't expect to find any virgins!'

As we approached Eagle Grove I could just make out the wharves of the port off to my left. Various ships were moored around the wooden jetties and plenty of activity was visible. Galveston was the main port of entry for all overseas visitors and the main destination for European immigrants. The city had become the largest in Texas with a population of thousands. The island itself was a narrow strip of land, sitting parallel with the coast of mainland Texas.

In the opinion of one of our number, Tobias Walker, who had spent some time as a labourer on the wharves, our best chance of obtaining powder was likely to be at a warehouse owned by one Samuel Williams. This worthy had established a commercial wharf at Twenty-Fourth Street back in '39. It was here that we hoped to fill our wagons with the finest Du Pont gunpowder, transported all the way from Pennsylvania in the United States of America.

With a thump, the ferry pulled in to the shore. Our brief sojourn was over. Returning to my wagon, I heaved myself up onto the bench seat, very conscious of the dead weight of the gold sovereigns stitched into my jacket. Those highly coveted coins had accompanied me across the Atlantic, on a misguided mission that had failed in all respects and left me as an unwilling deserter from Her Britannic Majesty's Armed Forces. Yet one man's loss is another man's gain and they were soon to be used in the purchase of much needed black powder destined for the beleaguered frontier settlement of San Antonio.

Once ashore, we clattered our way through the darkening streets. Even in the half-light it was obvious to me that Galveston was very different from the other Texas cities that I had visited. Although I had arrived there by steamer the previous year, my stay had been necessarily brief, and I had had nothing to compare it with. Now, as a seasoned traveller in the Republic, I saw things differently. The most noticeable thing to strike me was the lack of any apparent threat. Movement was uninhibited, laughter could be heard in the streets and the buildings showed no signs of fortification. It all confirmed the absence of the Comanche menace, which so blighted other parts of the country.

Having stabled the horses at a livery for much needed rest and feed, we walked through the wide streets. The buildings were a reassuring mixture of timber and brick. It was a balmy night and I felt strangely carefree, as though I was here at my leisure, rather than under orders from Texas's most revered ranger, Captain Jack Coffee Hays. He and I had struck a deal of sorts. I would fund the purchase of black powder and in return would receive a grant of land to put down roots with my lover, Sarah Fetterman. Unfortunately, the bargain would not be complete until the powder had actually reached San Antonio!

The hotel that Kirby had mentioned was a sturdy, square, two-storey brick building constructed six years earlier on the corner of Tremont Street and Post Office Street. The Twenty-Fourth Street Wharf could wait for another day. The night was ours to enjoy, or so I thought.

'Hot damn, will you look at all them candles? What the hell is that?'

I chuckled. The grizzled ranger known only as Travis was certainly impressed by our prospective accommodation.

'That's known as a chandelier,' I helpfully supplied, as we mounted the steps off the street into the lobby.

'Like staring into the sun,' he replied with childlike awe.

Only a short while later, Kirby and I, stationed side by side in our tin baths like monarchs on a dais, wallowed in steaming hot water as we puffed contentedly on our recently acquired cigars. Our clothes were being soundly thrashed by some flunky, in an attempt to extract the trail dust from them. With the prospect of an evening of wining and dining ahead of us, life seemed a little less hazardous.

My companion let out a joyful yell. 'Hot dang, I can't ever remember living this good. Probably because I ain't never have.'

I smiled contentedly as I nodded in agreement. 'Everybody deserves at least a taste of the good life and this little jolly is all courtesy of Her Britannic Majesty Queen Victoria, or at least her likeness on a coin.'

'Never met the bitch, but she'd get my vote!'

Surprisingly enough that made me chortle. A year or so ago I would have struck him, and called him out for such a comment. But now it really didn't seem to matter.

As the water finally began to lose its heat, we struggled out of the tubs and into our now, rather more respectable clothing. Ahead of us lay a veritable feast in the ground floor dining room, where such luminaries as Sam Houston and the current President, Anson Jones, had all been guests. Meeting the others downstairs, I was struck by just how much our appearance had altered in such a short space of time. Yet no amount of superficial pampering could hide the fact that I was in the company of seven very dangerous men.

Some two hours later, we all emerged bloated and merry from a truly gargantuan banquet. It was swiftly decided that we should all sally forth into an adjoining saloon catering to the hotel guests and others with the necessary currency to afford it. Kirby, who still had all of his wits about him, looked at me pointedly as he spoke.

'We'll all use our own specie for the liquor. Ain't no

9

sense in flashing those fancy coins of yours around for such as that.'

The saloon was a large room, easily capable of absorbing well over a hundred souls. Down one side there stretched a highly polished wooden counter with half a dozen barmen available to dispense drinks. The tables and chairs were all solid articles, some of the latter actually being upholstered. Around the room there were large mirrors affixed to the walls, mingling with some highly original signs such as: *No Discharging of Firearms on these Premises*, and *No Spitting on Floors*, to which some uneducated wag had added, *Or Ceelings*. Although it was nowhere near full to capacity, there were a few score occupants milling around in it.

Catching sight of myself in a mirror, I wondered what my former comrades of the Fourth Regiment of Foot would have made of me. Tall, just a tad under six foot, with broad shoulders and good posture, I still had a certain military bearing, but that was offset slightly by the unusual length of my dark hair and the distinctly casual nature of my clothes. There was also a certain hardness to my features and possibly an accentuation of my character lines that definitely hadn't existed before my arrival in the Republic.

My appearance and that of my companions obviously failed to repel certain ladies on the premises, as an enchanting array of fluttering lashes and heaving breasts soon surrounded us. A cynic could have asserted that it was more to do with our free spending, but whatever the reason they were a welcome sight. One female in particular appeared to have set her sights on me. Tall and well made, with lustrous dark hair and a slight cast in her left eye, she introduced herself as Vicky Fulsome. A cursory glance was sufficient to confirm that she more than lived up to her name. Unblemished skin, apparently good teeth and a figure tightly cinched in by corsetry all served to create a desirable impression. Which, of course, was entirely necessary for someone earning her living by bestowing sexual favours. For I was under no illusions that Miss Fulsome was a 'fast trick', a fact that did not detract from her appeal one bit. Her well-upholstered, highly prominent breasts seized my attention, pathetic male that I was, and she knew then that I was her mark for the night. Or so she envisaged.

'You're the best looking fella I've seen around these parts in many a day. How's about buying me a drink?'

Before I had time to even absorb that entrée she planted a lingering kiss full on my lips. If I had needed any confirmation that she was a common whore that sufficed in full, but nonetheless I found myself rather enjoying it. Enveloped by her seductive perfume I responded to her with enthusiasm, but just as I reached out to embrace her fully, a loud voice broke into my lusty concentration.

'Er, matey, how about another nip o' that brandy?'

The accent was undoubtedly English, which should not have come as any surprise. After all, I was in a port. Yet there was something about it, some intonation, which caught my attention. Establishing a proprietary grip on Vicky, I opened my eyes and twisted slightly to view the speaker. The man was angle-on at the counter a few feet away and with his back to me. He appeared to be of medium height, clad in the clothes of a working man. The barman's response had obviously been unsatisfactory, because his next words were of an altogether harsher variety.

'To the brim, you prick! I got money, see. Enough to buy this poxy flop 'ouse!'

In support of that assertion he slammed a coin down on the counter and my blood ran cold. The bartender looked suitably impressed, as well he might when beholding a gold sovereign.

Vicky drew back in surprise as she examined my face. 'You all right, mister? Looks like you done seen a ghost.'

Pulling myself together, I quietly replied, 'It's just been a while since I enjoyed the company of a lady. Perhaps you should arrange for some drinks, my dear. I would like to get to know you better.'

That and the coins that passed between us obviously satisfied her, as she gave me a lascivious smile and departed. Twisting around, I located Kirby and Travis seated at a table together. They appeared more interested in hard drinking than womanising and had shrugged off the lurking whores. Moving swiftly over to them, I hissed at Kirby, 'Do you see that character standing over there?'

Travis leered at me across the top of his bottle. 'Sworn off women and onto men, huh?'

Kirby looked at the man, but said nothing. He had noticed the urgency in my voice, and waited for me to continue.

'He's English and he just paid for his drink with a gold sovereign.'

Kirby peered at me keenly, understanding showing on his face, whereas Travis merely looked bemused. Cursing his slow wits, I hurriedly continued. 'Such a man is unlikely to carry gold on his person unless he has stolen it, or found a wealthy patron.'

'So what d'you intend doing about it, Major?' Kirby as ever cut straight to the chase. What was I going to do? The ranger's use of my now irrelevant title only served to highlight my problem.

Speaking with a certainty that I didn't really feel, I

answered firmly, 'When he leaves, I am going after him. I must find out who he is and what brings him here. There is always the possibility that he could be looking for me. You would do me a great service by observing anything that occurs after our departure.'

Travis blew through his lips like a horse, propelling whiskey fumes into my face. 'You're chasing shadows, fella. Go give that Dutch Gal a taste of your dick. She's mighty purdy.'

Kirby, on the other hand, nodded and replied, 'Reckon I can do that. Only don't go destroying anything. We've got business to tend to afore long.'

Smiling gratefully, I returned to where Vicky was pouring out our drinks. My quarry too had noticed her and was lecherously taking in the contours of her body, only slowly turning away when I returned. His lustful musings had given me time to see his face. With a scar running across both his top and lower lip, hard features and cold eyes, he could easily have fitted in to my old company of the 4th. But that didn't mean that he was a soldier or that I was his quarry. It would require some form of direct confrontation by me to discover that.

In a fever of impatience I sat with Vicky, sipping the so-called 'joy juice' and carefully watching him out of the corner of my eye. Her hand gently caressed my thigh, as she whispered innuendo into my ear. Sarah would have gone for me with a Bowie knife had she witnessed such a scene, but between Vicky and 'Scarface' I really did have enough on my mind. Just as her hand moved to my crotch, he pushed away from the counter and headed purposefully for the rear door. I could only imagine that he was making for the privy. With my wits feverishly struggling over a heady mixture of sexual stimulation and the tension associated with imminent action, I realized that I had to make

13

a decision. Whispering to her that I needed to relieve myself, I struggled to my feet.

'Hurry back, lover,' she called out throatily.

Wending my way around the outside of the room, I tried to see if anyone was paying me any particular interest. It did not seem so, but in that heaving throng it was hard to tell. Reaching the door, I passed swiftly through it and then closed it gently behind me. I found myself outside of the building proper, facing a large clapboard shack. From the foul odour emanating from it, my supposition had been correct. My intention was to catch my quarry whilst he was disadvantaged, so without further ado I proceeded inside. The building was split into two sections. On the right was a raised boardwalk leading to an earthen trench that served as a *pissoir*. To the left were three individual privies, with shoulder height wooden screens providing a modicum of privacy. It was all very grand compared with squatting in the earth, as was usual away from the towns.

I was in luck. 'Scarface' and I were the only two in the building. He was standing at the edge of the trench, noisily relieving himself. Without any hesitation, I unsheathed my hunting knife and strode up behind him. Up close he seemed of heavier build than I had earlier perceived. He displayed no alarm at my approach. In such a busy establishment there would be a constant flow of visitors. It was only as he sensed me immediately behind him that he began to turn, but by then it was too late.

Slamming my left boot into the back of his left knee, I followed up by smashing my knife hilt into the right side of his head. With an anguished groan he collapsed onto the damp boarding. Bending over him, I grabbed his lank, greasy hair with my left hand and brought the knife up under his chin, so that the well-honed blade nicked his Adam's apple.

'Can you hear me?'

His response to that was another groan, which at least confirmed that he was still conscious. Tightening my grip on his hair, I tried again. 'Answer me, or I'll cut into your gullet.'

This time he displayed remarkable clarity. 'I hear you, Your Honour. You be a fellow Englishman an' that's no error. So why the cutting tool?'

Ignoring the question, I again nicked his flesh, this time drawing blood. 'What brings you here? What is your business?'

His sour breath reached up to me as he answered. 'I'm an honest sailor, Your Honour. Fresh in from New Orleans this day. There's always work on this coast for an able seaman.'

Now I knew that he was lying. 'No ordinary seaman is paid in gold sovereigns,' I hissed. 'Who are you? Talk, or I'll cut you a new mouth!'

Pressing on with the blade, so that it actually sliced flesh, I left him with no illusions as to my intent and this time his reply confirmed all my worst fears.

'God's bones, you're out to kill me! Speirs. Cap'n Speirs brung me, along with four others.'

'Why?' I almost screamed the word, such was my agitated state.

'We're after some cove name of Collins. He's upset someone an' no mistake. Never seen the Cap'n with so much specie.' He wriggled to ease the pressure from my knife, but I countered this by pressing my knee into his back.

'So the sovereigns came from him?'

'That an' m—'

I never heard the rest. From behind me came a startled oath, as some gentleman unexpectedly walked in on a most unpleasant scene. Instinctively turning, I relaxed the pressure and it was all that my captive needed. Powering upwards, he thrust me back into a privy screen. It was built for modesty rather than strength and collapsed under my weight. Lying on my back, I kicked out with both legs and then swept the knife around in a wide arc. My opponent, for that was what he had become, had already rolled clear. Scrambling to my feet, I swiftly scanned the building. The individual who had discovered us had vanished, although whether permanently, or simply seeking assistance I knew not. My fellow countryman had pulled a long, narrow-bladed knife from his right boot. Watching me closely, he ignored the steady trickle of blood that was now staining his shirt. He had wisely decided that the single shot pistol in his belt was too cumbersome at such close quarters. I was in a similar situation. My Paterson Colt required cocking before it was ready to fire, so I too retained my knife.

'You're him, aren't you?'

Without taking my eyes off him, I gave a small bow. 'Thomas Collins at your service, and you would be?'

The other man sneered. 'Oh very posh, very correct. I *be* Sergeant Daniel Flaxton, *sir*. I never even *struck* an officer before, but one thing's for sure, I'm going to right enjoy killing me a major. Since it's all legal like, they might even give me a medal for it!'

Holding his gaze I replied, 'Many have tried,' and then did the exact opposite of what he would've been expecting. Stepping smartly backwards, I swiftly picked up the privy screen that I had collided with. It was thinly cut timber and not much of a shield, but it could serve to disguise my intentions. Gripping it in my left hand, I advanced steadily on Flaxton, who was warily observing my actions. Suddenly I rushed forward and threw the screen straight at the star- tled soldier. He had two options: to retreat, or stand his ground. He chose the wrong one and remaining rooted to the spot, savagely smashed the screen aside. As he did so, I dropped into a crouch and thrust my blade into his left thigh, twisting it viciously before withdrawing it. With a high-pitched scream he staggered back, slashing to left and right with his own knife. Fresh blood began to stain his trousers.

'You know, it doesn't have to be like this, Sergeant,' I called out softly.

The ugly scar twisted across his mouth as he spat out a response. 'You damned cockchafer, I'll slice you so your own whore mother won't recognize you!'

Throwing all caution to the wind, he launched himself towards me, but the nasty wound had served to slow him down. Shifting rapidly to my right, I then kicked out at his injured leg, catching him just above the knee. Unable to stop himself, Flaxton crashed face down onto the foul smelling boarding and lay there moaning in agony.

Twisting round, I threw my full weight on top of him, crushing any remaining breath from his lungs. Again I found myself gripping a clump of his lank hair, only this time I determined to finish the job. Yanking his head back, I placed my blade to his throat and .. . froze.

The keen edge was already drawing blood. I had him totally at my mercy, but I just couldn't do it. Apparently, the man was a serving soldier in the British Army. However reprehensible his task may have been, he was doing his duty as instructed. I could not, in all conscience, take his life.

Cursing myself for a damned fool, I released his hair. Upturning the knife, so that I was now gripping it by the reverse of the blade, I slammed the hilt down onto the sergeant's skull. Getting to my feet, I glanced down at his supine body. Whether the man survived or died was now up to him and any god that he chose to recognize.

Somehow I knew that I was going to regret my decision, but I also knew that I had to live by my rules, because to transgress would be the end of me.

Turning away, I sheathed my knife and walked cautiously out of the privy, absurdly aware that I hadn't even relieved myself.

CHAPTER TWO

Rapidly skirting the outside of the saloon, I arrived at the main entrance, reasoning that anyone watching the rear would be caught off guard. It also brought me closer to Kirby and Travis, whilst avoiding Vicky's undoubted charms. Having swiftly dusted myself off, I strolled nonchalantly, or so I hoped, into the large smoky room and sat down at their table. Travis's nose twitched and then he slammed the table, guffawing loudly.

'You were supposed to piss in the privy, not swim in it. Jesus, what a stink!'

Naïvely seeking confirmation, I looked over at Kirby and received an exaggerated shrug of the shoulders. 'You do smell a mite rank. And you've got some pilgrim's blood on your chin.'

Alarmed, I rubbed it on the inside of my sleeve. Could I really have expected to walk away from such a confrontation without displaying any sign of it?

Kirby smiled as he continued, 'You won't be the first fella to walk in here with blood on him, but mayhap it's time to leave. Unless you really intend poking that Dutch Gal.'

Travis staggered to his feet, shaking with a suppressed

mirth that was beginning to annoy me. Together we shouldered our way through the crowded room. Once outside, I asked Kirby if he had seen anything unusual at the rear of the saloon after I had left.

'One citizen rushed in looking like he'd just seen Christ on the cross. Whatever you was about in there, he wanted none of it.'

I related what had happened and the ranger raised his eyebrows. 'That sense of honour's gonna get you kilt one of these fine days. You'd better stay off the streets until we go for the powder. If that fella lives they'll know you're in the burg, but not where.'

Back in our bedroom the ranger became strangely withdrawn. Without another word he stripped down to his grubby underclothes and tumbled into bed. Dousing the oil lights, I too collapsed wearily onto mine, briefly wondering where our companions were. I looked across the room, through the darkness, to where Kirby lay. His breathing was regular, but I doubted that he was actually asleep. The soft mattress would be too much of a shock for him. It was a long time before I finally dropped off that night.

The unaccustomed noise of a busy thoroughfare awoke me early the next morning and immediately I was assailed by a multitude of unsettling thoughts. Amongst them was guilt at the memory of my enthusiastic response to Vicky's amorous caresses. Sarah might have remained in San Antonio, but she was clearly etched in my mind.

Stifling a groan, I clambered out of bed, poured cold water into a basin and doused my face. Only moderately refreshed, I turned to Kirby's bed, to find him wide-awake and scrutinizing me. From his mode of greeting he had evidently been conscious and pondering on our situation for some time.

'You notice anything wrong today, *any little thing at all,* and you holler. And make it good and loud, or you might not get the chance to give no two hollers. The powder means too much to us to let the British Army mess it all up! And if it comes to shooting, remember they might be your countrymen but they ain't your kin, so aim to kill.'

He was deadly serious, as was my reply. 'What concerns me is getting off this island with our wagons loaded with gunpowder. They'll make a lethal target.'

'And you'll be riding atop one of them, which is kind of fitting, considering this mess is all your making.'

The ranger had obviously been doing a lot of thinking. The fact that he was correct rankled, but at the same time I was beginning to get annoyed at the hostility that he was demonstrating towards me. 'Now see here, old boy, if it wasn't for my gold you wouldn't be here at all!'

'It ain't your gold. You stole it and now they're hunting you. And I ain't your boy!'

'My reasons for remaining in this country don't concern you, Ranger Kirby. Back in San Antonio, before I ever agreed to this undertaking, I warned Captain Hays that anyone pursuing me would arrive at this port. And do you know what he replied?'

Kirby eyed me warily, knowing that I was going to tell him anyway. 'He said, "Send them straight to hell, Thomas," and with or without your help, that's just what I intend to do. But without resorting to cold-blooded murder.'

The pitying look that accompanied his response showed just what he thought of my scruples. 'You're not playing some civilized game out here. If any of my men die through this, I'll hold you to account!'

And there we left it. It was too early in the day for a prolonged argument.

*

We were a strained and altogether different group as we gathered for breakfast that morning. The light-hearted anticipation of the previous evening had vanished. Travis was badly hungover. The habitually silent member of our party, Kirkham Shockley, maintained that pose. The other four had had varying degrees of success with the opposite sex. The ranger known as Frenchie was concerned that he might have contracted the pox.

'Was only when the bitch turned up the lamp that I saw the sores on her. Shit, I was out of there like a Pronghorn.'

'You'll have been moving too fast to get your money back then,' chided Tobias.

'Yeah, but was she *pretty*?' This from Ben Fielder who, from the tone in his voice, had not been fully satisfied by the previous night's activities.

Frenchie peered at him, bemused that his first description of her had not been sufficient. 'Oh yeah, *pretty* darned good at being ugly and *pretty* likely to stay that way!'

Swallowing a mouthful of coffee, I determined to bring our carriage back on track. Stabbing the table directly in front of Kirby with a forefinger, I said quietly but forcefully, 'If this mission is to succeed we all need to pull together, regardless of any change in circumstances. *It is what your captain would expect*!'

Jerking, as though I had slapped his face, Kirby fixed his hard eyes on mine for a long moment, before favouring me with a slow smile. 'You sure are a push hard, ain't you?'

No answer was expected or given and he slapped the tabletop, raising his voice slightly as he continued. 'Right, listen up, all of you. We go right ahead as planned, but the major here has got himself a problem. Maybe even five or six of them. And until we get the powder back to Béxar, they're also our problem, savvy? Thing is, as we don't know what they look like, they've got the first move. So we've got to be ready!'

The others absorbed his little speech, some of them looking decidedly puzzled. Not all of them had heard of my confrontation in the privy.

Out on the street, I held my shotgun cocked and pointing at the sky. My nerves were on edge, my palms were sweating and I was definitely beginning to regret not killing Flaxton while I had had the chance. The rangers spread out, so as not to present a closely packed target. My back felt clammy, far more than was warranted by the gentle sunshine. As we made our way through the streets of Galveston, I was aware of many curious glances from the various idlers and bystanders. Belatedly I realized that we were doing ourselves a disservice. Word was bound to spread of our heavily armed excursion. Glancing rapidly at Kirby, I instinctively knew that he had made the same judgement, for then he shrugged his shoulders, as if to say, 'What the hell else can we do?'

Finally we reached the stables. The teams were hitched and Travis and I clambered aboard. Clattering through the streets, I couldn't help but think how vulnerable we were to an ambuscade. Yet on the return journey we would be loaded down with the most dangerous man-made substance yet invented.

Transacting our business with Samuel Williams at his Twenty-Fourth Street wharf took remarkably little time. My gold sovereigns saw to that. Both wagons were soon fully loaded with a lethal cargo of Du Pont's fine grain gunpowder. Yet something had occurred that had caused me great concern. Williams, whilst happy to take my money, had been desperately reluctant *not* to hand over all his supply of powder. It had taken Kirby's threats of extreme violence to persuade him to accede to my demands. Thereafter, the ranger was too busy supervising the loading to give the matter much thought, but as we rattled our way towards the ferry I couldn't help but wonder just who it might be, that could have given the bulky, outspoken businessman the shakes.

CHAPTER THREE

Arriving at Eagle Grove for the return ferry ride, I received a not entirely unwelcome surprise. Standing there, large as life, was none other than the fragrant Miss Vicky Fulsome. She was clad in rather more sober attire than the previous night, but didn't appear any the less attractive for it. From the look of her stout boots and thick coat, she seemed prepared for a journey of some sort. The bulging carpet bag, partially concealed behind her, supported this impression. Beaming innocently up at me, she greeted me with, 'Well, well, if it ain't the handsome stranger. Hello, *lover.*'

The lean and moody Kirkham Shockley twisted sharply in his saddle to face me and snarled out, 'What's the whore doing here?'

Before I could answer, Travis fired off his own comment. 'Guess the British Army likes to travel with *all* its comforts.'

The others laughed, but Kirby snapped out, 'Button it, all of you. I don't believe this is the major's doing, is it?'

'Deuced right it isn't,' I returned indignantly. 'I have enough on my mind without adding to my woes.' Sharply I asked her, 'What just happens to bring you here?'

'Didn't realize I needed your leave to take a ferry ride. You fixing on taking the crossing as well then?'

'We have business elsewhere, ma'am, and short of

buying a ship, this is the only way off the island,' replied a sarcastic, but surprisingly eloquent Frenchie.

Vicky ignored him and instead settled her eyes on mine. 'Didn't think I'd be seeing you again. Took off kinda sudden, didn't you?'

Feeling ever so slightly embarrassed at having abandoned her, I chose to treat that as a statement and busied myself with leading the team onto the ferry.

Ignoring my rebuff she tried again. 'What you got in them barrels?'

Suddenly very conscious of Kirby's eyes on me, I knew that I had to think fast. 'Seeds for sowing,' I blurted out, grateful that we had tied stout tarpaulins over the barrels.

'Didn't take you fellas for farmers.'

'You ain't taken any of us yet, darling,' returned Travis with a leer.

'I got an age limit and you're well past it, old man,' Vicky spat back, obviously well used to handling men, both verbally and physically.

Whilst this repartee was going on, the other wagon was safely boarded and the rangers led their mounts onto the ferry. The ferrymen viewed our heavily laden wagons with dubious enthusiasm.

'You fellas weren't in town long,' commented the leader sourly.

'We like watching you work,' joked Davey Jackson, the youngest of the rangers.

Before the watermen could reply, Kirby added softly, 'So how's about taking the strain, if you want paying on this trip.'

Their leader seemed about to reply, but then thought better of it. There had been something in the ranger's voice that suggested the sooner they crossed over the better. Spitting a stream of tobacco juice over the side, he began heaving on the thick cable.

Gradually we began to leave the City of Galveston behind. Happy to gaze on the relatively tranquil water, I was at first unaware that Vicky was at my side. Turning to face her, I favoured her with a genuine and unforced smile. She really was most damnably attractive, whatever her profession. Yet surprisingly her expression was grave. Fixing her unblinking eyes on mine, she began to talk and what she had to say chilled me to the core.

'Whatever you fellas is up to don't matter two beans to me, but I kind of like you. Even if you did run out on me. It mayn't mean anything, but you ain't the first off the island this day. There was a pack of fellas travelled over come sunup and one of them spoke kind of funny, just like you.'

With my heart pounding, I asked her just one question. 'Was one of them wounded?'

Looking up at me warily, she nodded. 'Fella with a scar looked like he'd taken some real hard knocks. Was that you?'

Without answering, I turned swiftly away from my informant and sought out Kirby. As usual his searching eyes missed nothing. 'Looks like you done seen a ghost.'

The last person to say that to me had been Vicky Fulsome the previous night and things hadn't improved much since then. Conscious of the ferrymen nearby, I kept my voice low. 'You might not be far off the mark,' I said, and rapidly related the lady's revelation.

For once his self control slipped and his voice carried further than was prudent. 'Shit in a bucket! That just tears it. And here's us toting enough powder to. . . .' Realization hit, and his mouth closed like a hammer on an anvil, *but* the damage was done.

The leader of the ferrymen released the cable and

twisted round to face us, his florid, sweaty countenance flushed with anger as much as effort. '*Powder!* You done told the Dutch Gal them kegs held seeds.'

Pulling a knife from his right boot, he advanced on my wagon. Just as he reached it, Travis climbed onto the bench seat from the other side. His .36 calibre Paterson Colt was aimed unwaveringly at the other man's temple. With a cold smile he stated, 'You touch that stopper and I'll pop a cap on you. And it'll be in the head, so as not to damage the *seeds*. Savvy?'

'I thought rangers were supposed to be *peace* officers,' observed Vicky coquettishly.

The colour drained from the other man's face and he nodded dumbly. Nervously licking his lips, he slowly returned to the hawser where his two companions awaited him.

'And put that tarnal toad stabber back in your boot,' continued the ranger.

Regaining the initiative, Kirby bellowed out, 'Right, you sons of bitches. All three of you back to heaving on that rope. The sooner we're across, the sooner you're rid of us.' Turning back to me, he asked, 'If you was this captain sat over yonder awaiting on us, where would you be? In the shack, or back among the broken ground?'

Scrutinizing the terrain, I pondered the deployment of soldiery. A lot depended on their weaponry and skill in using it. I assumed that to be sent on such an extended mission they must all be like Sergeant Flaxton; tough, hardened and very experienced. They were unlikely to be equipped with smoothbore muskets. Therefore it was equally unlikely that they would be ensconced in the ferrymen's shack. If things turned against them they could be trapped inside the flimsy wooden building like rats in a trap. So it was very probable that they'd be positioned back from the shore, ready to utilize the greater range and accuracy of their rifles to pick us off, as we began our slow journey into the interior. The trail that we were to follow wended through broken ground, with heavy vegetation and groves of trees of a kind that I did not recognize.

The two wagons, crammed as they were with gunpowder, presented us with a terrible dilemma. If Speirs knew what they carried, he could finish us all with one volley. But did his orders encompass the slaughter of Texan nationals?

I decided that the best course was for us to disembark quite normally and then leave the wagons by the shore. The rangers could fire a volley and we would all take cover around, but not inside, the shack awaiting developments.

Abruptly ending my deliberations, I returned to Kirby's side and shared my thoughts with him.

After hearing me out he replied, 'Your druthers are my druthers, Major.'

Keeping their backs to the shoreline, the rangers drew their revolvers and cocked them in readiness, eliciting alarmed looks from the three ferrymen. Vicky had noticed our preparations and I put a question to her. 'If you were abroad so early, why did you not cross with the other group?'

I watched her intently as she replied, trying to ignore the cast in her left eye that so added to her allure. 'There was something about them fellas that made me nervous. They looked like plug-uglies and mean with it.'

'And we don't?'

'When you've been around men long as I have, you get to notice the differences. You and your friends look like a bunch of hard cases, but you don't give me the shivers.' Then she added coyly, 'Except when you kiss me.'

Her answer sounded authentic, or at least most of it did, but I didn't have time to ponder the more pleasant aspect of it. The ferry was now very close to Virginia Point. '*Stay here!*' I commanded. 'Until I say otherwise.'

The heavy wooden structure slammed into the short jetty far harder than expected, heralding our return to the mainland. The ferrymen wanted rid of us, of that there could be no doubt. As they tethered the primitive craft to the support posts, Travis and I clambered up onto our respective wagons. The six rangers led their horses off and then mounted up, their movements purposefully unhurried and natural.

Finally we had the wagons on *terra firma* and it was time. Reining in, I applied the brake, and then leapt off the seat clutching my shotgun. Kirby and the others aimed their revolvers at the broken ground beyond the shack and each discharged one chamber. The relative peace of the morning was roughly shattered by the crashing report. Before the smoke had time to clear they had veered off to the right and reached the ferrymen's dilapidated abode. It occurred to me, as I ran to join them, that we were going to feel very foolish if all this came to nought.

There was a sharp crack some twenty odd yards away and Ben Fielder spun round like a ballerina. Somewhat unnecessarily Kirby yelled out, 'Hit the dirt. We smoked 'em!'

Strangely enough my first thought was for Vicky, standing out in the open on the ferry. Rising up off the ground, I shouted at her, 'Get down, *now!*'

Thankfully she had sufficient presence of mind to dash off the craft, where there was little cover, and drop to the ground amongst thick vegetation.

The ferrymen's first reaction to the sound of gunfire was

to stand and gawp, but on noticing that Ben had stopped a ball, they rapidly decided that the delights of Galveston held a great deal more appeal than those of the mainland. Frantically they heaved on the gnarled hawser. Even as they did so, I realized that they were making a dreadful mistake.

'Watch for the smoke,' I bellowed.

As if to order, three shots rang out and smoke drifted up, marking the positions of the hidden marksmen. Their combined accuracy was quite remarkable. All the straining figures were struck simultaneously. Two slumped to the deck. The other was thrown off the craft by the projectile's momentum and promptly disappeared under the waves.

'Shit in a bucket, that's fine shooting,' commented Tobias softly. And yet one of the three was still alive. Bleeding profusely, he should have remained still, but pain had robbed him of his wits and he began to crawl blindly across the deck. One more shot rang out and the wounded man's head appeared to explode, as a large calibre ball smashed into and then out of it, taking skull fragments and brain matter with it.

There then followed one of those eerie moments of total silence, when even the horses refrained from making any noise. Keeping low, I took the opportunity to view our dispositions. Ben appeared only to have sustained a flesh wound and was receiving rudimentary first aid from young Davey near the far side of the shack. The other five rangers were spread out in the prone position, aiming their long rifles towards to the most recent sighting of powder smoke. There was little point in returning fire, as any skirmisher worth his salt would know to move after each shot.

'Looks like we got us a standoff here,' remarked Kirby grimly.

'Except that they're not after you, only me,' I replied, 'and now that I've purchased the powder, I'm surplus to requirements. So if you wished to, you could hand me over and ride off.'

The other man turned to look at me, incredulity etched on his face. 'You got a mighty cheerful take on life, ain't you?' He stared at me hard for a few seconds before speaking again. 'There's three reasons why that don't answer. You and the captain made a deal, and I ain't about to break that. Them bastards done holed one of my men and I aim to settle with them for it. And lastly, I don't know what you do in the god damn British Army, but out here we don't abandon our own.'

I felt genuinely touched by that last comment and was about to thank him, when a hail from across the way interrupted me. At the same time a white shirt appeared, tied to the muzzle end of a rifle.

'I say, would one of you gentlemen be Major Thomas Collins, late of the 4th?' The speaker had adopted a languid tone, the like of which I had not heard for many months. Under different circumstances I would have welcomed the sound of a fellow officer.

I cautiously raised myself a few inches off the ground, very conscious of the deadly skill of those opposing me. 'You must be Captain Speirs. I have heard a great deal about you.' A little embellishment could do no harm, if it caused him to wonder just how much his subordinate had told me whilst under my knife.

Taking my reply as our acceptance of the flag of truce, a tall figure now rose up from amongst a grove of trees some twenty-five yards away. He had dark hair, broad shoulders and from his posture appeared quite relaxed with the situation. My companions shifted their aim slightly, but held their fire.

Showing no concern at this, Speirs said, 'From my standpoint that's rather disappointing, but no matter. The main thing is that I have found you.'

'You will understand if I don't share your enthusiasm,' I retorted.

Kirby, growing impatient, hissed at me, 'Enough of this shit. Let's just drop him and be on our way.'

Speirs nodded his head slowly, although whether this was in response to my comment or some other I was unsure. Appearing to come to a decision he called out, 'Major, might I suggest that we honour the spirit of the truce, and come together for a private discussion? I give you my word as a gentleman that you have nothing to fear.'

I shook my head emphatically before replying. 'I have nothing to gain and everything to lose, by stepping out into the open with you. I have no experience of the value of your word, but the way in which you dispatched those three unfortunates demonstrated that you are totally ruthless.'

He was too far off for me to see his eyes, but the sneer on his face was all too evident. 'Ah yes, well, that was a shame, but I couldn't allow them to raise the alarm. With the ferry immobilized there can be no interruptions from the city.'

I glanced down at Kirby. This discourse was not leading anywhere constructive. Then came the question that I had dreaded. 'Might I ask what you are transporting in those wagons? Only it seems a little unusual for a field officer to be riding atop such a thing, like a common carter.'

My pulse quickened, as my mind raced to think up a plausible reply. The captain had obviously not visited Williams's warehouse during the hours of darkness and therefore could not know the nature of our cargo. I gave a tight smile and said as smoothly as possible, 'It cannot have escaped your notice that I am no longer a serving officer in Her Majesty's Army. I am now a man of business and that merchandise belongs to me.'

The speed of his response confirmed that Speirs obviously had an agile mind. 'I can't believe that you would stoop so low as to involve yourself in trade, but no matter. Whatever you are transporting must have great value, if you require an escort of seven Texas Rangers.'

'That is nothing unusual,' I swiftly answered. 'As a new arrival here you may not know that this country is regularly scourged by groups of heathen savages known as Comanches. Lone travellers are most vulnerable to attack and only. . . .' Speirs never heard the remainder of that sentence, as off to my right there was a sudden flurry of gunshots. It would be hard to say which of us dropped to the ground first, but his own withdrawal was encouraged by the discharge of Kirby's rifle.

'The lick-spittle's tried to flank us,' he bellowed at me.

'That's because Kirkham tried to flank them,' observed Travis. 'So much for the god damned truce!'

'And we now know that they are quite prepared to kill Texans to achieve their aim,' I offered. 'That being the case we somehow need to overwhelm them, or at least get past them.'

Travis spat into the earth before saying forcefully, 'Long as we're hauling them wagons, we've got no chance of outrunning them.'

'So we end it here, now!' There was a hard, calculating tone to Kirby's voice that was quite chilling. Years of hunting and fighting Comanches had imbued him with certain qualities, rarely found even in a professional soldier. However I did have two advantages over him: I had an idea how to end it, and I also possessed the means.

CHAPTER FOUR

'Jesus! You don't mess around, do you?'

I had just informed the duo that we were going to explode a keg of gunpowder in amongst Speirs and his men. Travis provided the colourful prose, whereas Kirby immediately questioned the plan.

'And how do we get it there without someone suffering real bad?'

This was the part I knew they would not be keen on. 'We strap it to a horse, send it straight for them, and ignite the powder in their midst.'

That was too much for Travis. Rising up, he stabbed a finger at me and yelled, 'You're not blowing up my horse, mister!'

A shot rang out, and a ball slammed into the shack just behind him. Cursing, he dropped back to the ground, uncomfortably aware of the splinters embedded in his jacket. I looked questioningly at Kirby. He at least had not rejected my plan. Focusing on me, he demanded, 'Right, two questions. Whose horse were you figuring on, and how do we blow the keg?'

Ignoring the deeply sceptical Travis, I came straight back at him. 'Ben is wounded, not seriously, but enough to slow him down, so he can ride the wagon next to me.'

Travis couldn't contain himself. 'Oh, he'll just love that. You having just exploded his horse and all!'

Kirby snapped back, 'You got a better idea? Either put up, or shut up!'

Ignoring their exchange I continued, 'For the bomb to be really effective, we need to empty out some of the powder, then replace it with pistol balls, and any other bits of metal we can find. That way, if you and your rangers volley fire at the keg, there should be enough metal striking metal to provide the spark that we need.'

Kirby was watching me intently. 'You really got it all thought out, ain't you?'

Conscious of just how thin my plan really was, I favoured him with a broad smile. 'I must have done something right, for so many people to want me dead.'

Slapping his thigh, he gave a genuinely hearty laugh. 'I can see why Jack Hays likes you. Right, it's your plan, so get moving. We'll cover you best we can whilst you get the powder.'

Thereby lay the rub in any master plan. Someone had to carry it out!

Crawling back towards the wagons, I had not attracted any fire. I would be most vulnerable when I attempted to remove a keg. It was highly unlikely that Speirs would believe that I was now some kind of frontier shopkeeper. If the British soldiers opened fire the whole supply could go up. '*British soldiers*'! It was hard to believe that I was actually under attack from my own kind.

I was on the point of reaching up, when a voice called out to me.

'What in tarnation's happening?'

Twisting around, I found myself facing a very agitated Vicky Fulsome. Since instructing her to take cover, I had given her no thought, but her sudden appearance gave me an idea. 'Get out of that coat and walk slowly out in front of this wagon.'

'Why?' Encouragingly, the tone of her reply showed a degree of curiosity.

'Because even those bastards are unlikely to shoot at an extremely attractive young woman and I need their attention diverted whilst I remove one of these kegs.'

She appeared quite taken by my 'attractive young' description, and quickly divested herself of the topcoat. 'And a glimpse of your legs wouldn't go amiss, miss,' I added with a broad smile. 'A very generous glimpse!'

She obviously had leanings towards a career on the stage, because she rose up slowly and began to parade up and down in front of the wagons, as though innocently taking the air. Not one discharge greeted her display, which was entirely understandable. She wore a tight, form fitting burgundy coloured dress, which hung down to her ankles. Under the entirely false pretext of boggy ground, she had shamelessly hoisted this up above her knees, treating anyone who cared to look, to the sight of two well-turned calves.

Leaping up, I thrust my hand under the tarpaulin and took hold of the nearest small keg. I had to get well away from the wagons before Speirs recognized the deception and opened fire.

Awkwardly holding the container on my right shoulder, I charged across the open ground towards the cover of the shack. Realization had finally dawned. Shots rang out and large calibre lead balls thwacked into the ground. With a loud shriek, Vicky dropped to the earth, her seductive promenade abruptly concluded.

Chest heaving, I threw myself down at the rear of the shack next to Ben and Davey. Rapidly I ordered them to fill their powder horns from my container and to do the same for the others. Once everybody's was full, there would be a sizeable space available. Next I packed rifle balls and a selection of nails found inside the shack, into the keg, before pressing down the stopper. I was well aware that I had created a truly lethal cocktail.

Kirby was still sprawled out in front of the building, intermittently returning fire, so I called out that all was ready. Next came the most unpleasant part of the whole undertaking. Travis produced a coil of rope, also from inside the shack. The saddle was removed from Ben's horse, as it would have added insult to injury for him to lose that as well. Careful to keep our clandestine activities out of sight, we firmly tied the keg onto the animal's back.

Grabbing its forelock, Kirby led it to the side of the building. His six rangers, for even the wounded Ben was included, cocked their revolvers. Standing ready with my sawn off shotgun, I was greatly surprised to see that Kirby was aiming his weapon at the horse.

'*Now*,' he yelled and with a crash all six revolvers discharged in unison. Smoke wreathed about our position so that, for a vital moment, Ben's horse was obscured. Kirby placed the muzzle of his revolver on its rump, and squeezed the trigger. The emerging ball gouged a bloody furrow through its flesh. With a scream of pure agony, partially masked by a second volley from the rangers, the demented creature leapt forward, and careered towards Speirs and his men.

Swiftly the rangers discarded their handguns. Grabbing their long rifles, they took careful aim at the fast receding horse. Seven men were targeting one small wooden keg and all knew that a successful outcome depended solely on their accuracy. At least one ball had to penetrate, and strike metal at just the right time. Not possessing a rifle, I was spared the strain imposed by such a task. Instead I was poised to break into a run with my 'two shoot' gun.

The 'pain' that Kirby had visited on Ben's horse had placed it in a world of its own. The unfortunate animal appeared to be trying to outrun the anguish engulfing its hindquarters and mercifully in the right direction.

'*FIRE!*'

Executing a perfect volley, seven rifles crashed out as one and I was off through the rolling smoke. With a truly awesome boom, the tightly packed powder keg exploded. From somewhere ahead came a high-pitched scream. Something tugged at my sleeve and I prayed that the rangers were close behind me.

Chest heaving, I reached the uneven ground with its grove of trees and vegetation. Whatever awaited us, it was for me alone to discover.

The sight that greeted me was far worse than any slaughterhouse, because human beings were involved. Ben's sacrificial horse no longer existed. It had quite simply disintegrated. The trees, festooned with entrails, were fairly dripping blood. Bizarrely, two of the animal's severed legs were lying on the ground at an angle of forty-five degrees, as though marking the way ahead. Something that had once been a man, lay near the source of the blast, his features obliterated, yet still clutching a now buckled and useless rifle.

But the dead, however gruesome, presented no threat. Those still living were another matter, and I had the shotgun tucked tightly into my shoulder, as I searched intently for any movement. All my senses were on alert as I cautiously moved deeper into the trees.

My heart leapt as, off to my right, I heard the metallic click of a hammer being pulled back. Galvanized into action, I twisted around, fired off one barrel and raced forward through the sulphurous smoke. Ears ringing from the concussion, I searched frantically for my foe. The undergrowth was desperately thick. I should have been hugging the earth, rather than blundering around searching for an unseen enemy. My whole body crawled with tension, whilst my torso was clammy with sweat.

'*Christ!*' Mere inches before me gaped a rifle muzzle, and for a fleeting instant I foresaw my own death. Instinctively I swung the shotgun stock around, the butt connecting with the long barrel. The rifle fell from lifeless fingers and I beheld another British soldier, albeit not in uniform, slumped against a tree, blood seeping from multiple wounds. Gazing into dull, half-lidded eyes, I drew a deep breath and shuddered.

From somewhere close, Travis's voice bawled out, 'Hit the dirt,' and I threw myself to the ground. A ball slewed into the earth mere inches away, and then there was a volley of shots from the rear. That resulted in a high-pitched scream, followed by a flurry of oaths.

My companions were now level with me, and I got shakily to my feet. No matter how many times I came under fire, I was never entirely free of some reaction to it.

'You did good, fella,' commented Tobias Walker from off to my left. It was the last thing that he was to say in his short life. From some yards away there was a strange ignition, and a volley of shot flew at us. Tobias uttered a strangled cry and tumbled backwards. Taken aback by the unexpected broadside, we all dropped to the ground. Up ahead there came the sound of horses' hoofs milling around, as men mounted up.

Speirs's unmistakeably cultured voice called out to us. 'The field is yours, Major Collins. I underestimated you this time. Be assured I will not make that mistake again!'

With that he wheeled his horse around and with one

other companion, galloped off into the hinterland. As the hoof beats receded, an eerie silence settled over the killing ground. Faint wisps of smoke lingered in the undergrowth, as though reluctant to finally disperse. From the detonation of the powder keg to Speirs's enforced departure, only a handful of minutes had passed. Making an elementary calculation I called out to the others, 'There must be four of his men remaining hereabouts and I have seen but two.'

'We done holed one over yonder,' yelled Travis. 'We'd best spread out until we find the other.'

The dark and brooding Kirkham Shockley answered softly, 'No need, there's bits of one back there apiece.'

Turning to look down at Tobias, I was shocked to see that he had been hit twice instantaneously. Once in the throat, and again in the temple.

Kirby was also studying the body. 'One of them was packing some kind of volley gun.'

A thought occurred to me. 'I believe it to be a Pepperbox. In England it is regarded as an officer's weapon.'

The Pepperbox was the world's first true revolver and pre-dated Samuel Colt's invention by several years. Rapid fire was possible, as the hammer did not require cocking before each shot. Unfortunately the gun had a reputation for unreliability and was notorious for discharging all six barrels at once.

Travis spat a stream of tobacco juice. 'Whatever it was, that cocksucker's gonna pay!'

'*God almighty! What have you done?*'

The genuine unrestrained horror was so evident in Vicky's voice that we all turned to face her. Obviously feeling safer with us than lying next to two wagons full of powder, she had followed on at a discreet distance, but was now clearly regretting her decision.

I moved towards her, intent on offering some comfort. Hardened as I was to bloodshed, I had forgotten what it was like to witness such carnage for the first time.

Screaming at me to keep away, she drew a single shot, muzzle loading derringer from her purse and vaguely threatened the six of us with it. She was clearly over-wrought and acting on impulse, but no less dangerous because of it. Although highly inaccurate due to its lack of barrel length, her weapon was of .40 calibre and at such close range could very easily kill anything that it hit.

Aware of Shockley moving silently down the flank, I began cautiously inching forward. Pointing the small pistol directly at me, she howled out for me to stay back. All her frenzied attention was on me and that was all the ranger needed. Running flat out, he collided heavily with her, wrenched the derringer from her hand and gave her an open handed slap across the face.

'These work better if you cock them first, you afflicted bitch,' he commented acidly, as she collapsed to the ground.

'There was no call to hit her,' cried out young Davey angrily. 'She was just having a conniption fit.'

Shockley settled his cold, hard eyes onto the youth and snarled, 'Nobody points an iron at me. *Nobody*!'

Davey wilted under the verbal assault, but still had the guts to reply. 'But she's a lady.'

'She's a whore. Belongs right where she is, on her back!' With that he turned, and stalked off without a backward glance *but* he kept the derringer.

The shock of the blow, rather than any associated pain, appeared to bring Vicky to her senses. Without making any effort to get up she lay there before me, showing a deal more leg than was ladylike.

'Well, don't just stand there gawking,' she complained,

'help me up. Or are you like the animal that just left?'

'I believe you know that I'm not,' I answered, reaching down for her hand. Accepting it, she held on tightly as I heaved her upright. Feigning loss of balance, she fell forward into my arms and remained there, as though to steady herself. Although highly susceptible to a woman's charms, I was not a complete buffoon. Smiling down at her I said, 'You are an exceptionally attractive lady, Miss Fulsome, but you should be aware that I am not a blithering idiot. I can tell when someone is overacting. You should also know that I am romantically attached and not about to jeopardize that.'

She stepped back slightly, and gave me an appraising look. 'Then she's a lucky woman, whoever she might be.'

Kirby's loud voice interrupted any further discourse. 'If you're through jaw boning, we got some tough calls to make. Figure you might want to contribute.'

If I detected a note of sarcasm, I didn't show it. But his next remark jolted me to the core. Indicating Tobias's lifeless body he snarled, 'And think on this. He's dead because you couldn't see to business in the shithouse. It happens again, you and I are gonna have a serious disagreement. Savvy?'

Recovering from my surprise, I came back at him fiercely. 'And if you had need to kill a ranger in cold blood, could you do it?'

The two of us were now face to face, eyes locked together, the tension almost palpable between us. I knew that grief and anger played a large part in his verbal attack on me, but years of exercising military authority had left me unable to tolerate such behaviour. Thankfully the irreverent ranger Travis effectively broke the spell.

'You two can stand around here eyeing each other all you want, but someone needs to see to them wagons.'

Gratefully turning away from his leader, I joined him and the other rangers and we all walked slowly back to the landing place. When asked by Frenchie if they were to place Tobias under the sod, Kirby replied sadly but firmly, 'We ain't got the time, so he stays where he lays.'

Nearing the shoreline, I became aware that we were being watched by dozens of people across the channel at Eagle Grove. The explosion, along with an unusual amount of gunfire, had attracted the attention of the Galveston citizenry. From the shouts and gesticulations, they obviously wanted their ferry back. Kirby ignored them completely, remaining deep in thought until we reached the shack. Motioning for us all to gather round, he began speaking.

'Tobias is dead. There ain't nothing gonna bring him back, but we can make all this mean something by getting the damn powder back to Béxar. Way I figure it, them two fellas out there won't try that again, because they don't know which trail we're taking. They'll try to keep us in sight and wait for a chance.'

'What about the islanders, and the dead ferrymen, Kirby?' This from Frenchie.

'The hell with them fellas! By the time they get a boat over here and find this mess, we'll be long gone.'

Suddenly I saw it all so clearly. 'But we won't be travelling together all the way, will we?'

Kirby's eyes locked onto mine and he smiled. He had obviously pushed our recent difference of opinion to the back of his mind.

'What the hell's he mean by that?' Travis looked at the two of us, confusion registering on his face.

Kirby continued regarding me as he commented, 'You really ought to join the ranger force, Major. This is in your blood.' Turning to the others, he continued, 'What he means is, we'll be splitting up. Moving slow like this, if a Comanche war party jumps us, we're finished. If we're in two groups, taking separate trails, at least one wagon should make it.'

Grim as ever, Shockley voiced what everyone was thinking. 'That's suicide for whoever draws the short straw!'

Kirby was unyielding in his reply. 'That's as maybe, but it doubles our chances of getting some powder back to the captain.'

Travis spewed black juice before speaking. 'And I suppose you already worked out who goes where, ain't you?'

Nodding gravely, Kirby replied, 'Yup. Kirkham and Davey with the major, the others with me. If it weren't for the major, there'd be no powder. It's his spondulix that paid for it. Kirkham, you got a problem with any of this?'

Their eyes locked, and they regarded each other for long seconds. Finally the other man took a deep breath, and a faint smile crossed his face as he answered. 'It's your call. Jack Hays set you above us with good reason. As for the Redcoat, well, I'll stand with any man that'll fight the Comanche.'

So there we had it. I was to lead one group, and Kirby the other. Looking out across the water I had cause to remark, 'Then I suggest we all charge our weapons and depart. They seem to have summoned the Navy over there.' Across at Eagle Grove, a large rowing boat filled with men was beginning to make its slow journey towards us.

'Just you wait a god damn minute,' came an angry female voice. 'What about me?'

Kirby regarded Vicky dispassionately. 'What about you?'

A mixture of fear and exasperation showed on her face. 'You can't just leave me with all these dead bodies.'

Kirby, obviously considering the whole conversation a low priority, had begun reloading the discharged chambers of his revolver, but his reply was well reasoned. 'Not one of them fellas is gonna think you had a hand in this. Just tell them the truth, *and go back to Galveston*. Flash your titties, and you'll no doubt get the ride for free! Which is more than I ever do, ha ha ha.'

The others laughed along with him, but something troubled me. There was an air of desperation about Vicky, which was confirmed by her next comment. 'I need to go to San Antonio. Take me with you, *please*.'

Travis had had enough. 'Lady, there's going to be more dying on this trip. You don't want to be anywhere near us.'

'What is so important about getting to San Antonio?' Pressingly aware that we needed to be off, I was nonetheless curious.

'I need to find my cousin. I've been told by some freighters that she lives there now.'

Feeling strangely light headed, I asked, 'What's this lady's name?'

'Sarah Fetterman,' came the reply.

CHAPTER FIVE

'Get on!'

'Say what?'

'Get on the blasted wagon, unless you want to answer to them,' I shouted, indicating the approaching boat. 'If we're here when they arrive, there'll be hell to pay.'

So saying, I grabbed her coat and bundled her up onto the bench seat. Taking hold of her carpet bag I, none too gently, hurled that up after her, before climbing on myself. Shockley gave me a piercing look but remained silent. With much creaking and vibration, we slowly pulled away from Virginia Point, to the accompaniment of howls of protest, and poorly aimed gunfire from the occupants of the rowing boat.

Some hours travelling found us well clear of the coast. We had not yet gone our separate ways, as there was little like-lihood of us encountering any savages this early in the journey. What *was* becoming apparent, was that this return trek would be far lengthier, and more arduous, than our journey out to Galveston. Both wagons were heavily laden, and great care had to be taken to avoid potholes.

Shockley was out of sight, ranging far and wide, but his

overly harsh treatment of Vicky stayed in my mind. I determined that there would have to be a reckoning of sorts, which in itself was disturbing. It suggested that I had developed a protective attraction to her and such situations rarely remained platonic. That lady seemed content to sit silently next to me, as the wagon bumped and jolted its way northwest. Under other circumstances I would have welcomed my close proximity to such a comely wench, but the state of affairs had drastically altered. Touching her arm, I tackled the subject that had so surprised me. 'If you are Sarah's cousin why has she never made mention of you?'

Vicky turned and spoke softly, so that I had to strain to hear over the noise of our progress. 'Why should she? She ain't seen hide nor hair of me in years. I didn't want a life of toil on a farm. I wanted pretty dresses and a soft bed.'

Watching her carefully I said, 'But it wasn't that easy, was it?'

'No. No it weren't. I got the dresses and the bed, but every man I met wanted me out of them and into it.' Putting her hand on my arm, she smiled. 'And they weren't all like you. Many were ugly, smelly, stunted oafs from Morgan's schooners, who thought spondulix got them anything!'

'You know nothing about me,' I replied quickly.

'I know what I see, and hear. They're enough for a woman who knows what to look for.' As she said this she pressed closer to me on the seat. Under different circumstances I would have revelled in the intimacy, *but she was Sarah's cousin, for God's sake!*

This has to stop, I thought reluctantly. Shifting uncomfortably I asked, 'How did you know of our destination, and why go there now?'

'Some of your ranger friends supped too much joy juice. What they said got me to thinking that maybe I could hitch a ride. Sarah's steady and sensible. Might be she'll help me settle down.' Arching her eyebrows she added, 'And I'll get to see more of you too!'

I just didn't like what I was hearing. Vicky Fulsome appeared to be an opportunist, albeit a highly delectable one. The thought of taking on two women at once, although superficially appealing on a physical level, augured terrible trouble. Especially when they were related. So it was with genuine relief that I saw Kirkham Shockley return to the wagons, his appearance serving to divert our attention. The light was draining out of the sky and the taciturn ranger brought news of a suitable camp-site up ahead. It was on higher ground, and clear of vegetation, making it easier to defend.

Kirby ordered a cold camp. It was unlikely that Comanches would be so close to the coast, but somewhere out there Captain Speirs and his sergeant were lurking, biding their time. As we sat near the wagons chewing beef jerky and dry biscuits, I remarked pointedly, 'I say, Kirkham, whilst we are all here together, I would be grateful if you would return Miss Fulsome's property.'

His head snapped up. 'Say what?'

Young Davey froze in the midst of chewing, so that his face resembled that of a man afflicted with lockjaw. The hitherto quiet camp fell totally silent as everybody awaited the turn of events.

'You retained her derringer,' I persisted. 'It is likely that we will encounter Comanches on our journey, so she'll need it for protection.'

'That bitch aimed to pop a cap on me. I ain't giving her any second chances!'

'You won't have to,' I replied evenly. 'You have my guarantee that there will be no recurrence. Besides, it was not you alone that she threatened with it.'

49

'Your fancy words don't mean shit to me,' Shockley snarled, his hand drifting closer to the butt of his revolver.

Suddenly, from out of the gloom, Kirby began talking in an almost conversational tone. 'Trying to recall that night on the Brazos. When was it? Five, six month ago?'

I stayed silent, as was expected and he carried on. 'The night you sank that dang steamer. What was it, the Mustang?'

A nod signified my agreement.

'How many men got killed that night, Major?'

Without taking my eyes off Shockley I answered, 'Seven!'

A wary look had crept over that man's face, as he registered the import of the strange conversation.

'Hear tell you used a scattergun on most of them,' continued Kirby inexorably.

Something approaching alarm was now registering on Shockley's countenance, as his eyes flitted to the coat at my side. Kirby fell silent, knowing full well that he had said enough. As Shockley and I maintained eye contact the tension in the camp increased. I was aware of Vicky inching away from me. Sensible girl, I thought, as her action gave me an idea to augment the pressure. Softly I said, 'A little more.'

Still seated on the ground, she shuffled a bit further away.

'A little more,' I repeated, knowing exactly the effect it would have on the man opposite. Encouraging her to move away seemingly invited him to start something.

Shockley was a hard, stubborn and bigoted individual, but he had sense enough to know when to back down. I had caught him off balance. With a resigned sigh, he slowly reached into a jacket pocket and withdrew Vicky's 'purse cannon'. Leaning forward he gently placed it on the ground before him. Then, clearly lacking the good grace to easily accept the situation he got to his feet, collected his rifle and moved off.

Kirby called out to him, 'Think on this, Kirkham. We got troubles enough out here, but the major ain't one of them. Don't go turning this into more than it is.'

The other man briefly glanced over his shoulder, before fading into the darkness. In the gloom nobody had been able to observe his expression.

Kirby slapped his thigh as he remarked, 'That's one hard man to read. Weren't sure whether he was gonna call the bluff or not.'

Throwing my coat to the side, I lifted my shotgun for all to see. 'It was never a bluff!'

Travis guffawed with mirth. 'Hot dang! I can see why they made you an officer.'

'Well, actually they didn't,' I replied with a smile. 'My father purchased the original Commission for me as a way of accommodating a second son. But I take your meaning, and thank you for the compliment.'

For once even Travis was speechless!

For the next five days we continued steadily west. That would remain our heading, now that we had reached a similar latitude to our destination. The sun had just reached its highest point of the day, when our slow progress suffered an unexpected interruption. Shockley, his lean face impassive as ever, rode swiftly to our front, and motioned for us to stop. The sudden lack of noise and movement was almost unsettling, after the relentless hours spent on that bench seat. Dropping down to the ground, I twisted and stretched, wondering what could have brought him back amongst us so rapidly.

'We got company! Around a dozen Anglos all loaded for

bear. Look to have been riding real hard from the coast.'

Kirby's puzzlement was obvious. 'Didn't think they'd pursue us over them killings.'

'Maybe them watermen had family thereabouts,' remarked Frenchie softly. 'Kin can be funny about such things.'

Recalling Williams's sweaty nervousness in the warehouse I spoke up. 'It makes very clear sense if it's about the powder.'

Kirby looked at me nonplussed, unusually slow to comprehend.

'Do you not recall the extreme disquiet on that merchant's face,' I continued, 'when he realized that we wanted it all? Someone had already laid a claim.'

Recognition showed on the ranger's face. 'Dang it to hell, we don't need this. How long we got, Kirkham?'

'About time to take a shit,' the other man answered.

'We should use the wagons as shelter,' I ventured. 'If I'm right, they won't want anything to happen to these barrels any more than we do.'

'That's one hell of a gamble,' he replied sharply, but nonetheless instructed us all to take cover behind them.

We had hardly made our dispositions before there came a thunder of shod hoofs and our pursuers hove into view. On seeing that they were discovered they abruptly reined in.

'Mother of God,' Vicky gasped, 'they look like ghosts!'

It was hard to disagree; such was the quantity of trail dust coating the horsemen. They had ridden long and hard to catch us, but now that they had, they seemed undecided as to their course of action. A pitched battle, centred on two wagons packed full of gunpowder, must have seemed distinctly unappealing.

All six rangers had their long rifles cocked and ready,

whilst I held my shotgun in the crook of my arm. Taking advantage of the temporary lull, I carefully viewed our surroundings, and quickly realized that neither side had any territorial advantage. We were situated at the bottom of a very gentle grassy slope, with neither trees nor any substantial vegetation near us. The gradient was so slight as to cancel out any real benefit to the others, if they should attempt a charge. I could not immediately make out any significant cover if we were to abandon the wagons, so there was nothing for it but to hold fast, and wait on events.

Our pursuers, sitting their horses some seventy-five yards away, had obviously come to the conclusion that there might be some benefit from a parley, as one of their number advanced slightly and dismounted, carefully avoiding any sudden moves. Arms spread wide, almost in supplication, he shouted over to us, 'Hot dang, but ain't you a sight for sore eyes? You made good time from Galveston. I'm right proud of you.'

Travis muttered under his breath, 'What the hell's he rabbiting on about?'

'My name is Jacob Sutter,' continued the spokesman. 'I'd deem it an honour to parley with the boss dog of your outfit.'

Kirby stepped out from behind the lead wagon and advanced two paces, rifle pointing skyward, but still cocked. 'Reckon that'd be me, but I won't be closing the gap any.'

'Fair enough, friend, fair enough,' replied Sutter conversationally. Even at that distance he was an incongruous looking character. His large frame was encased by a long frock coat. He had a substantial beard, although this was partially covered by a voluminous scarf that he used to hold a stovepipe hat in place. I could not imagine why anyone would choose to wear such headgear on horseback. Almost as if he had overheard my thoughts, he slowly reached up to remove it. 'Now the thing is, we've ridden awful hard to catch up with you folks, on account of what took place at Virginia Point. Not saying you're to blame though, no siree, not saying that at all. But there has to be a reckoning, back in Galveston in front of the General.'

'By Christ, that's all we need,' I muttered to no one in particular. Calling softly over to Kirby I said, 'Ask him which General. If it's Lamar, it means he is after some or all of this powder, and he won't rest until he gets it.' My skin crawled at the thought of that man's involvement. Many of the trials and tribulations that had confronted me when I first arrived in the Republic were due to his chicanery.

The ranger shouted back, 'I don't know any Generals. Who you got in mind?'

'His Honour the former President Mirabeau Lamar of course, the saviour of this glorious nation.'

The man obviously had a blinkered view of his patron, but that made everything suddenly so clear and it definitely explained Williams's nervous reaction to our demand for all his powder stock.

Kirby, however, showed little sign of being impressed. 'You need to back up some, Mr Blowhard, else there'll be blood spilt. First off you ain't interested in us; it's these barrels you're really after. And the thing is, they belong to Captain Jack Hays of the San Antonio Ranger Company. So you can follow us all over God's creation, but you ain't laying a hand on them. As for the ferrymen, they were all shot by some English soldiery.'

'We found them in the trees, or at least bits of them. Massacred to a man,' returned Sutter accusingly.

'I ain't no god damn massacree,' howled a deeply

54

offended Travis, stepping up next to his leader. That man ignored him, and responded in an altogether calmer fashion.

'Them assassins were killed legal, in self defence and I'll swear to that before Captain Hays himself in Béxar County.'

'So you fellas are all Texas Rangers then?'

Hesitating slightly, Kirby managed to resist the temptation to look back at me, before answering boldly, 'Every damn one of us!'

This response was met with silence, as Jacob Sutter struggled to evaluate the situation. If he tried to rush us on horseback, he would undoubtedly lose the majority of his men. On the other hand if he started a firefight, he could easily ignite the powder and kill us all. Either way he could not justify going into battle against Texas's finest. Even on the coast he must have heard of the rightly famous exploits of Captain John Coffee Hays, defending the land against Comanche depredations.

Recalling the attempted flanking movements at Virginia Point, I took the opportunity to search the surrounding countryside. Sutter could possibly have sent some men circling around behind us. I was aware of Vicky, crouched down behind my wagon, looking curiously up at me. She probably considered it odd that I should be looking away from the assembled horsemen. Turning a full 360 degrees, I couldn't see anything out of the ordinary. And yet an uneasy feeling had settled on me.

Letting my eyes drift back to Sutter, I was suddenly aware of a small cloud of dust mushrooming up from his long tailcoat. Then he staggered back, as though struck by some invisible force. Almost simultaneously, blood gushed from Kirby's neck and with a loud groan he collapsed onto his knees. Instinctively taking in the angle of the ranger's wound, I looked off to my right and sure enough, at the crest of a small knoll some 200 yards away, there lingered a telltale puff of smoke.

CHAPTER SIX

'*Tarnal assassins,*' screamed out Travis, as he discharged his long rifle at Sutter's men. *Exactly as it was intended he should.* Davey rushed over to Kirby, grabbed him under the armpits, and heaved him to the rear. Shockley, although oblivious to the real origin of the deadly rifle balls, had the presence of mind to bellow at his comrades to scatter away from the powder wagons. Half carrying their leader, five men and one terrified female scurried off to their left. This allowed them a clear field of fire at the Galveston men, who at this point were milling about in confusion.

I, on the other hand, did the exact opposite. Gripping the heavy shotgun tightly in my right hand, I drew the Paterson Colt with my left, and ran towards the remaining wisps of smoke as though the hounds of hell were after me. Somewhere up ahead I knew I would find Captain Speirs and Sergeant Flaxton.

Realizing that it was impossible to reach them before they reloaded, I zigzagged wildly in the hope of confusing their aim, and as a consequence gave myself further to travel. Frantic exertion produced torrents of sweat. My heart began to thump heavily. Every nerve end was alive. I expected to receive a stunning blow at any moment. But when it did come, it had the most unusual consequences.

Having just completed another dogleg turn, I witnessed a burst of smoke some fifty yards ahead of me. Simultaneously, the shotgun received a brutal jarring contact and was sent spinning from my hand. It crashed to the ground off to my left, and with a roar both barrels discharged. Providence was surely with me, as the lethal hail flew directly at my two adversaries. At that range the expanding spread of projectiles was unlikely to prove deadly to the prone men, but it did have the effect of disrupting their aim. My breathing was becoming laboured, and my legs felt like lead, but I *was* nearing their position.

And then I saw him. Sergeant Daniel Flaxton cocked his rifle, and calmly took aim directly at me. Swiftly raising my revolver, I squeezed the retractable trigger. With my right hand still numb from the vicious blow it had suffered, I had retained the Colt in my left and as a consequence my aim was off. As the weapon roared, I saw earth fly up directly before Flaxton's muzzle at the very moment that he fired. A sound resembling that of a bee in flight swept past my left ear. Gasping for breath, I burst into their lair.

The two men had discovered a small hollow in the ground, which had proved perfect for some long range sniping. Flaxton's visage loomed up at me, as he struggled to his feet. The deep knife wound to his left leg was obviously a major impediment. Without any scruples, I levelled my piece at his torso and again squeezed the trigger. The weapon belched forth smoke, and my opponent disappeared from view. Then, further back and to my right, I saw the man that I really wanted.

Captain Speirs was desperately trying to wipe fresh blood from his eyes, fully aware of my presence but unable to react. One of the projectiles from my shotgun had gashed his scalp. It was not a serious wound, but he was bleeding profusely. As I stood there, revolver again at the ready, he clamped a soiled handkerchief to the injury. The captain appeared to accept my sudden ascendancy, as he made no attempt at resistance.

This was the first time that I had seen him at close quarters. Underneath the grime and blood he was undeniably good looking, but there was a hint of cruelty in his dark features, and maybe something else. His lips were a little too thin, his chin a little too finely honed. Finally able to look me up and down, Speirs favoured me with a sardonic smile. 'Damn, but you must be the luckiest fellow living to have survived three encounters with my men and I.'

Now that we were no longer creating our own din, I became aware of continuing gunfire from the two embattled groups below us. My first priority was to get my prisoner down there, to demonstrate that they were skirmishing unnecessarily. Speirs's rifle was lying safely out of reach, so I gestured with my revolver.

'The Pepperbox. Place it on the ground where I can see it, but slowly. It has already killed one of my companions.'

The other man shrugged. '*C'est la vie*, as the Frogs would say. For me too, it has been a costly excursion.' As he spoke his dark eyes suddenly seemed to glitter with renewed vitality, as though something had just changed.

'*Flaxton!*'

Something solid collided with my left knee, causing my leg to buckle under me. If I had dropped my revolver at that point I would have been finished. As it was, now lying on my back, I found myself staring directly up into the six muzzles of a Pepperbox! In sheer desperation I squeezed the trigger. The charge detonated and the ball flew off into the blue yonder, leaving me with only two chambers to defend myself.

Speirs responded in kind, but under duress his aim was

no better than mine and the ball thumped into the ground near to my left shoulder. Frantically I rolled twice to my right, before getting to my knees. The captain had tried to follow my movements, but was again struggling to peer through the blood flowing down from his scalp wound. Again I fired and this time the ball tugged at his jacket sleeve.

One chamber remaining!

With a howl of sheer frustration he twisted away, and ran pell mell for his horse. The animal was ground-tethered at the reverse foot of the knoll. Holding my weapon, this time with both hands, I cocked the hammer and took careful and deliberate aim. Sighting down the barrel onto the centre of Speirs's broad back, I took a deep breath and squeezed the trigger. There was a loud pop as the percussion cap detonated and then nothing . . . *Hang fire!*

'God damn your eyes,' I cried out after him in dismay.

Blasphemy appeared to be my only remaining weapon. My revolver was, to all practical intents and purposes, now empty, but might still be dangerous. Taking care to keep it well away from me, I watched helplessly as my target released the reins, clambered into the saddle and sped away. It appeared that I was not the only one to lead a charmed life.

From behind me came Flaxton's mocking voice. 'Just can't quite finish the job, can you, *Major Collins*?' Helplessly sprawled on his back like an overturned turtle, he tried to laugh, but all he could manage to produce was a red froth bubbling up out of his mouth. This matched the liquid seeping from the hole in his chest. Kicking out at me had clearly used up all of his remaining strength.

Dismissing Speirs from my mind, I walked slowly over to him, ensuring that my revolver again pointed in his direction. He was unarmed and seemingly near to death.

Although panting for breath and obviously in great pain, he still managed to sneer up at me. 'You've had your five. That barker's empty!'

As though acknowledging the fact, I let my weapon drop to the ground and reached down to grasp one of the two discarded rifles. Coughing up a gobbet of slime, he regarded me mockingly. 'You're a toff, you haven't got the guts.'

Glancing swiftly at the nipple, I couldn't see a copper cap, which meant that the muzzle loader had been discharged. No comfort there! Looking down at Flaxton's scarred and yet strangely vulnerable face, I steeled myself for the inevitable. Because of my misplaced sense of honour, one or more of the rangers had died and it could even have been his ball that struck Kirby. Reversing the rifle, I stood over the mortally wounded soldier and raised my arms, so that the metal clad butt was directly over his head. I saw real fear in his eyes for the first time and my limbs began to tremble as I steeled myself to deliver the *coup de grâce*. Mistaking this reaction for hesitation he spat out, 'I'm a screamer!'

Hardening my heart I replied, 'Good for you,' and brought the butt down on his temple with a sickening crunch. Any sound that he was about to make was choked off immediately. Not content with a single blow, I struck again and again. It was as though some form of blood lust had come over me, which had to be purged from my system. Then, quite abruptly, it just dissipated. All strength left my body, and I found myself slumped on the ground next to Flaxton's now barely recognizable corpse. The rifle stock was coated with brain matter and hair and I threw the weapon from me in disgust. The uncomfortable realization hit me that I was now no better than the man that I had just bludgeoned to death.

As though a fog was drifting clear, I gradually became aware of the outside world. Gunfire was emanating from both groups. It was up to me to make the peace. To do that, I would have to provide Lamar's men with proof that the rangers had not instigated the bloodshed.

Having no intention of going down amongst them unarmed, I reloaded the Paterson Colt. It was a laborious task which resisted most attempts at speed. Then, tucking the weapon in the back of my trousers, I took hold of Flaxton's body by the ankles and dragged him out of the hollow onto the slope facing the combatants. His head was now a stomach churning pulp, which I could no longer bring myself to look on.

Tipping him over, I pulled off his jacket, then his waistcoat and finally what had once been a white shirt. The stink of body odour and most noticeably urine, drifted up from his unwashed torso, indicating the extent of his fear in those last moments. Tying the bloodied article around the stock of the other rifle, I hopefully had a recognizable symbol of parley. Taking hold of the barrel with both hands, I set off slowly down the slope towards the Galveston men. Viewing them with a critical eye for the first time, I noticed that two men had retired a further hundred yards with all the horses and that the rest of them were making themselves small by hugging the earth. With the advantage of height, I could see that Sutter lay where he had fallen and was, at the very least, seriously hurt.

So engrossed were the two groups in trying to kill each other that I must have covered at least one hundred yards before my approach was noticed. With every step, my sense of foreboding had increased. I was convinced that in their present mood someone must surely take a shot at me. My shirt, already clammy from my exertions, was now a wet rag as the tension within me increased. I became aware that the firing on both sides had died out, as all attention was transferred to my steady approach. A voice bawled out from the band of rangers.

'What in tarnation are you about?'

Ignoring Travis, I continued steadily towards the other group. It was their reaction that concerned me and it was not long in coming.

'Whoa, mister! You're mighty brave or mighty stupid, but either way you just stop right there!'

I did as instructed. Their distrust of my intentions was quite obvious, as a goodly number of rifles were pointing directly at me. I had to gain some measure of credence in their minds, as it only took one tense, sweaty forefinger to end my life. In a loud, clear voice I stated my case. 'We did not shoot Sutter! If you look behind me. . . .'

Crack!

Something slammed into a stone next to my right foot, whilst before me smoke drifted over the assembled men. My heart leapt in reaction, but I knew exactly what they were about. It was a test. If the marksman had intended to hit me, I would most assuredly have been laid out, with a hole in my temple. Ignoring the source of the shot, I turned towards the rangers, and frantically waved my 'flag'.

'Don't shoot. For God's sake, hold your fire!'

In response Vicky screamed out, 'Get down, you madman. They'll kill you for sure!'

'They won't unless you open fire,' I replied, before turning back to face the Galveston contingent. 'If you look up on the slope behind me, you will see a body. That is one of two men that fired on both parties. The other has escaped, but in any event he is no longer a threat to you. It is me alone that he seeks.'

With that I rested my case and stood in silence awaiting their verdict. It was not long in coming. The earlier spokesman clambered to his feet over the protests of his companions. 'Move in closer, mister. Keep your hands where we can see them. You've got grit, I'll give you that.'

Relief flooded over me and I carefully made my way down to join them. Not surprisingly, I was faced with a mostly sullen and dispirited group of men. Their leader, Jacob Sutter, remained where he had fallen, his coat by now drenched with blood.

'Dead as a wagon tyre,' commented the only other man standing, shaking his head sadly. He was a bearded, long faced individual, who already seemed to be feeling the burden of his new position. Having led men in many situations, I knew exactly how they were all feeling. Fired up by Lamar into an enthusiastic pursuit, they had lost their commander in the first encounter. Whoever then took over was unlikely to have as much influence over them.

Scratching his head, their new chief viewed his recumbent troops in exasperation. 'Land sakes, get on your dang feet. It's over. Chet, you and Teal get up that slope and make sure that fella's dead.'

The two designated individuals got reluctantly to their feet and cautiously headed towards Flaxton's body. Their leader soon felt it necessary to shout after them, 'If you don't get moving, he'll start to turn.'

Conscious of my aching arms, I asked if I might lower the flag of truce. The other man viewed me shrewdly before nodding acquiescence. 'Only don't go reaching for that iron tucked in your trousers.'

For some minutes we regarded each other in silence, as neither of us felt any inclination towards small talk. Consequently it was with some relief that I greeted the return of his men. One of the two assumed the role of spokesman. 'He's mustered out all right, what's left of him.'

Looking dubiously over at me, he continued, 'Jesus, mister, you must have really took against him.'

Now that it was obvious to me that there would be no further outbreak of aggression, the whole situation was becoming a deuced bore. Fixing the young man with a steady gaze I replied, 'He attempted to kill me, that was reason enough.'

I was saved from any further interrogation by the cautious arrival of both Travis and Frenchie. 'We done brawling then or what?' asked the former. Without awaiting a reply he continued, 'The powder stays with us, unless you want more empty saddles.'

The Galveston men had plainly had enough bloodshed. Their leader said, 'You're free to go. There weren't supposed to be any killing.'

'Tell that to *His Honour* the General when you see him,' retorted Travis as we cautiously retreated. For some time we walked awkwardly backwards, careful to keep our erstwhile enemies in full view at all times.

'How is Kirby?' Having seen the ball strike, I was expecting the worst.

'Not good,' said Frenchie. 'The ball passed right through, but he's lost a passel of blood and can't speak. Whether he lives or dies, he's out of it.'

That was indeed bad news. Kirby was the glue that held us all together. All the men liked and respected him. With Speirs still out there, things were looking decidedly bleak.

CHAPTER SEVEN

At least one person was demonstrably happy with my safe return. Rushing up to me, Vicky threw her arms around me in a disconcertingly familiar fashion. 'Thomas, I thought you was a goner for sure.' Her full moist lips attached themselves firmly to mine and it was some time before I could disentangle myself. As I reluctantly struggled free she breathlessly remarked, '*Cher*, you take too many risks. What if you'd been kilt?'

'That's right,' I answered pointedly, 'What *would* have become of you?'

Pulling free, I looked around for Kirby. Ben, himself still recovering from the wound received at Virginia Point, was kneeling next to his supine figure. He had tied some cloth tightly around his leader's neck in an attempt to staunch the flow of blood, but it was clearly not working. He was coughing continuously, so as to avoid choking on the sticky liquid. Ben's eyes met mine, and he gave a barely perceptible shake of his head. Softly he remarked, 'This won't answer. Even with a sawbones, I don't know that he'd make it. The ball entered just below the jawbone and went out t'other side. That hole's bigger, and just won't plug.'

'Let me see,' I said, bending down to release the soiled bandage. As the cloth fell away, I knew immediately that if anything were to be done, it would have to be quickly. The entry wound was clean and could heal, but the ball had become disfigured before exiting the left side, making that hole larger. The torn flesh had little hope of knitting together unassisted, and the level of blood loss could not be allowed to continue.

Getting to my feet, I peered around at the assembled rangers. 'If we move this man as he is, or just stand by and do nothing he will surely die. I have no medical experience, but I once witnessed something that may save him. Whatever your opinion is of me, I think that you owe it to him to give me the chance.'

Davey asked what everybody else was thinking, 'How do we know it'll work?'

In reply I was blunt, brutal even. 'I don't know that it will. He could even expire under the knife, but at least we will have tried. *Or we could just leave him to die!*'

With a start I felt my ankle being nudged. It was all Kirby could do to attract my attention. Dropping to my knees, our eyes met as he desperately tried to talk. Leaning closer, I gasped as his right hand closed on my wrist like a vice. As spots of blood hit my face, he was just able to mouth two words, '*Do it!*' Then his hand fell away.

That was all the confirmation that I needed. Galvanized into activity I leapt to my feet.

'Right, I need a fire making here. Davey, be so kind as to collect the kindling. I'll also need hot water, and something for him to bite down on. Ben, let me have a blanket to place under his head. Oh and I'll need some whiskey to cleanse the wound.'

Unsurprisingly nobody moved. Faced with a barrage of orders from a foreigner, who wasn't even a ranger, they all remained rooted to the spot. In exasperation I bellowed out, 'If you want this man to survive do as I say, or you will all answer to Captain Hays.'

Unexpectedly, Kirkham Shockley was the first to move. Prodding Davey he directed, 'C'mon, you heard the man. Let's get the makings.' The youngster knew better than to argue and so together they went off in search of wood. That was enough to bring everybody round. Speed being of the essence, Travis produced one of his carefully hoarded Lucifers with which to start the fire.

With everybody working together we soon had a roaring fire and a pan of water heating up over it. Accepting that I would be the one to carry out the unpleasant task, I had placed my broad bladed knife into the hottest part of the fire. As the metal heated, Ben and Frenchie placed a rolled up blanket under Kirby's head and prepared to hold him down. Travis and Kirkham were to take his legs, but then Vicky surprised me by volunteering to hold Kirby's hands, rightly thinking that he might be comforted by her presence. Her under-slip had been shredded to form lengthy bandages and these were dropped in the pan to boil clean.

Finally everything was ready. Pulling the cork stopper out of the whiskey keg that Travis had produced, I remarked, 'This is purely for medicinal purposes,' and took a long swallow. The fiery liquid careered down my throat, before hitting my empty stomach with a jolt. Cheap and nasty it may have been, but it provided me with some much-needed 'Dutch courage'.

'Shit or bust, Major,' Travis returned, with a disturbing air of finality.

My knifepoint was glowing red as I withdrew it from the embers. Nodding to the others, I commanded, 'Hold him fast.'

Ben placed his knife hilt between his leader's teeth and then, along with Frenchie, pressed down on the man's shoulders. Kirby locked eyes with Vicky and stared at her unblinkingly. She favoured him with a gentle smile and gripped his hands tightly.

Firmly moving his head to give clear access to the vivid injury, I positioned the glowing blade directly above it, took a deep breath and pressed down hard. With a strangled roar the ranger bucked and twisted so violently that it required the combined strength of all those present to hold him in place. Flecks of blood covered Vicky's face, but she held fast, continuing to gaze deep into her patient's anguished eyes. Tears were coursing down her cheeks from the pressure of his agonized grip. Desperate though I was to release him from his private misery, my instinct told me to maintain the pressure, so giving the flesh time to fuse.

'He's had enough, mister,' cried out Davey, grabbing hold of my arm.

I hung on grimly, as the sickly sweet smell of burning flesh pervaded the atmosphere. With a sigh, Kirby passed into blessed unconsciousness and then suddenly it was all over. Throwing the blade away, as though accursed, I grabbed the raw alcohol and spilled it over the cauterised tissue. This provoked a slight tremor but nothing more. Easing her bruised hands from his, Vicky retrieved my knife, and used it to haul out one of the makeshift bandages from the pan. Drained by the ordeal, I could do no more than observe, as she allowed it to cool slightly before wrapping it tightly around Kirby's neck. The four men had released their grip, and sat around looking strangely self-conscious.

The coming of darkness found us all sitting around the dying embers of the fire. We had, of necessity, lingered at the same site for the remainder of the day. Kirby was totally unfit to travel and would remain so for the foreseeable future. Since the makeshift operation he had not stirred, but his breathing seemed a little easier. His survival was out of our hands, dependent mostly on his iron constitution and the passage of time.

Taking advantage of the roaring fire, the whole group had dined on hot pinto beans wrapped in tortillas and supped piping hot coffee. The hot meal had improved our spirits, and so for a time there was a genuinely companionable atmosphere present amongst us. It was as though Kirby's injury had somehow brought us together in common cause.

But then, as the cheerful glow receded, more sober thoughts intruded. From now on there could be no more fires during the dark hours. Somewhere out there Speirs would be waiting for another opportunity to strike. He had proven himself to be a resourceful and inventive officer, and presumably stood to gain much from my capture or verified death. And looming before us, like some dreaded pestilence, lurked the ubiquitous Comanche menace. All of which meant that there were decisions to be taken that night.

First and foremost was the appointment of a new leader, but thereby lay a problem. I knew that the task was quite within my capabilities, but also that I could not put myself forward. So when the subject was raised I remained silent. As expected it was Travis, garrulous and lacking in any sensitivity who got the ball rolling.

'Kirby's well out of it, but somebody's gotta call the shots.'

'You putting yourself up for it then, *Travis*?' This from Shockley, with just the hint of a sneer.

'No, I ain't, *Kirkham*,' he replied with vigour.

These two, although totally different in temperament, were the strongest personalities in the group. It was left to Vicky to state the obvious. 'Well, even if you sad bunch can't see the wood for the trees, I surely can!'

To a man, the rangers turned to face her. Undaunted she continued, 'You don't need no schooling to realize Thomas is your man. Face it, for Christ's sake!'

The others looked at each other, but remarkably nobody gainsaid her. Typically Travis summed up the mood.

'Way I see it, he's been an officer in some man's Army, which is more than any of us have amounted to. And he put up the money for the powder.'

'Put it to a vote,' added Vicky slyly.

Shockley spat on the embers in disgust. 'We don't need all that shit! You got the job, Mr Collins, Major or whatever the hell else you call yourself. Just don't mess up!'

My first command decision would be immensely painful, and was to have unforeseen results. 'Whatever transpires with Kirby, he is plainly unfit to travel. Yet tomorrow we must move on. One of us should stay behind to tend him. Do I have any volunteers?'

Surprisingly Shockley was first to speak. 'I ain't sure what "transpires" means, but however you look at it we need all the guns we got for the journey. I say the Dutch Gal stays with him. If he lives, he might just get lucky.'

Vicky glared at him. 'Why can't you ever call me by my given name? It ain't too hard to remember, even for you!'

I could see some practical merit in his idea, but it was devoid of all feeling and conscience, so my rebuttal of it was swift. 'I cannot accept that. Whether he lives or dies, Vicky would be left to fend for herself, easy prey for any Comanche war party.'

Travis eyed me speculatively. 'You sure there ain't some other reason?'

'No, there isn't,' I answered firmly and without the elaboration that he was seeking. 'So I need a volunteer to stay here for as long as is needed. Who shall it be?'

To my surprise Frenchie was quick to speak up. 'Don't reckon I've got any choice. Him and me's distant kin. Can't leave him out here for the varmints to chew on.'

So it was agreed. He would remain behind as guardian and possibly gravedigger. Which took us down to five men and one woman against a proven killer and however many Comanches that we might possibly encounter.

After such a gruelling day, I was more than ready to stand down and snatch a little sleep. The night watch was split into three shifts of two men, with me forming half of the final one. Vicky had elected to tend Kirby when required; a none too onerous task, as he remained unconscious. I had little reason to afford her any thought as I rolled into my blanket. With Kirkham and Davey having drawn the first shift, the other three had gratefully surrendered to temporary oblivion. The heavy cloud had cancelled out whatever moon there was, and the darkness seemed complete. The silence was broken only by the occasional murmurings and grunts from the rangers' erstwhile leader, as he lay on the cusp of life and death. I reflected gloomily that he was only in such a parlous state because of his association with me, which did little to hasten my descent into sleep.

Never having mastered the soldier's art of dropping off in any conditions, I lay on the hard ground, only slowly drifting away. Yet in time I had so completely relaxed, that her fingers on my face almost caused me to cry out. Heart pounding, I grabbed for my revolver, only desisting after hearing her whisper.

'Shh, *cher*, calm yourself. There's no danger this night, only pleasure.'

Mind befuddled, I did not immediately comprehend her meaning. Only as she began to stroke my hair and nuzzle me, did I realize what she was about.

'Those bastards were out to leave me here, but you stopped them. Now I'm gonna thank you properly.'

A hand slipped under the blanket, and with the speed born of much practice, undid the buttons of my trousers. Suddenly picturing Sarah looming over me, incandescent with rage at my infidelity, I tried to brush her away.

'This cannot be,' I whispered hoarsely. 'You are Sarah's cousin. Besides, our coupling could not escape unnoticed.' So there it was! In my heart I had already accepted my need for her.

In any event she would not be denied. 'This ain't Béxar, and she ain't here,' she stated flatly. 'Land sakes, man, we might not even make it back there.'

As if emphasizing those words, her hand tightened around my manhood and abruptly all was lost. Maintaining a highly charged silence we made love swiftly, as though both realizing that time was of the essence. Afterwards I was barely able to control an enormous sigh.

As if in a fantasy she whispered in my ear, 'So now you're mine, *cher bebe*!' With that she turned away, and crawled carefully back to Kirby's inert form.

It was not until some time had passed, with the first watch having nearly run its course that I was capable of reflecting on the *full* content of Vicky's last words to me. She had announced her possession of me in no uncertain terms, and in circumstances that could only bode ill for the future. Whoever had coined the phrase, 'the frailty of women' did not know that gender very well.

CHAPTER EIGHT

As the new day emerged, I gazed upon our little encampment. My eyes settled briefly on Kirby's prone figure, and I was assailed by feelings of guilt. I did not relish the thought of leaving him behind. He had proved to be a capable leader of men and wise to the ways of the world. But as Travis had stated the previous day, he was out of it. It was now up to me to see us back. Even with only five men remaining we would still have to press ahead with the plan to split the group, as we would have no hope of fending off a determined Indian attack. Whichever party might be discovered first would face almost certain annihilation, whilst with luck the others should make it home. Which suggested that, by agreeing to stay behind, Frenchie was definitely more intelligent than he looked. Whether Kirby lived or died, he would in all probability be able to follow on unhindered.

That thought led me onto Vicky's presence in our midst. Her chances of actually meeting her cousin again were looking slim. I could have insisted that she remain with Frenchie, but I was under no illusions as to his morals. To complicate the situation further, thoughts of her extremely accomplished seduction kept intruding. That suggested that she could well have succeeded in her 'so now you're

74

mine' strategy. Which of course brought Sarah unwittingly into a *ménage à trios*.

My descent into madness was postponed by the realization that the camp had now come to life, and that the pickets could safely withdraw. Approaching the site from opposite directions, Travis and I gratefully tramped back to join the others and there chewed pensively on some strips of beef jerky. With the notable exception of Miss Fulsome we were an unusually subdued group that morning, all of us aware that, for one reason or another, we were unlikely to see Kirby again. Vicky, on the contrary, seemed to be savouring a private triumph and favoured me with many a broad smile as she went about her tasks.

Our erstwhile leader had survived the night and was now appearing to drift in and out of consciousness. He was desperately weak and likely to remain so for some time, if he survived. Anxious not to prolong the parting, I gave out my first instruction of the day.

'It is time we left this unhappy spot. Frenchie, I wish you only good fortune and very much hope to see you and your patient back in San Antonio before long.'

The other four rangers also said their farewells, but they seemed somehow restrained, as though they too had grasped that their companion might well be benefiting from the arrangement. As though an invisible line had been drawn, that man now collected his belongings and stationed himself close to Kirby's recumbent form.

The irrepressible Travis couldn't resist firing off a parting comment. 'Keep your pecker hard and your powder dry, pardner!'

The rest of us mounted up in silence. Vicky climbed up onto the bench seat and sat close to me, ensuring that her thigh was in contact with mine. Groaning inwardly, I reflected that lust could be both a pleasure and a cross to bear. Whatever the eventual outcome, it was going to be a very long journey indeed.

Looking back, for possibly the fourth time, I discovered with a slight shock that the two men had finally blended into the distance and were no longer visible to the naked eye. So that was it. Kirby and Frenchie were on their own and we continued on our way, shadowed I was sure by the potent wrath of Captain Speirs. A combination of greed and anger was certain to be keeping him somewhere in our rear. Knowing that there would be an experienced outrider circling the party, he would hang well back, which would effectively keep him beyond rifle range of me. He would probably be unaware, as I had been the previous year, just how much danger he might be in from the Comanches.

So deep in thought was I that the sudden placing of a hand on my thigh made me jump.

'Damn it all, woman, you startled me!'

Vicky's face betrayed a certain wounded nervousness and she hastily pulled back. Reproachfully she answered, 'I thought you liked my hand down there. None of these others would turn me away.'

Slightly chastened, I had to acknowledge the truth of that. 'I do, and so would they. Which is the very reason why you must keep your distance. I cannot, must not, allow your presence to create any ill feeling amongst us all. My leadership of them is not yet on a firm footing and we could, *all of us*, be in very great danger soon.'

Vicky's undeniably delightful face clouded, as she took in my words. 'I saw what you did to that fella back there. It ain't over with them either, is it?'

'To my knowledge there's one left, but I believe he's the most dangerous. And when we split up, as we must, he'll be behind us with Comanches possibly up ahead.'

'I've never seen them, but I've heard tales,' she replied dubiously.

I responded in deadly earnest. 'You must never allow yourself to be seized by them. *Never!* Do you understand?'

Every drop of colour drained from her face as realization struck home. 'That's why you made Shockley return my Derringer. You think I might have to kill myself, don't you?'

'There is that possibility. In any event you must be alert to your surroundings. Don't ever wander off by yourself.'

From the strained silence that greeted that advice, I knew that she was rattled.

For the next two days we slogged laboriously westward, all the time praying that the fine weather would hold out, at least until we had forded the wide Colorado River. Once across that, I intended that we would split up into two parties. At that point we would well and truly be in the hands of fate.

Finally, shortly before noon, on the third day after leaving Kirby, we beheld a line of trees in the distance. That could only mean we had reached the Colorado. The river stretched from the coast up to Austin, the official capital of the Republic and on into the interior. Once across, we would have a vast tract of open ground ahead of us.

Somehow sensing the liquid, the horses pulled strongly and soon we were faced with a whole vista of trees and water stretching off in either direction as far as the eye could see. Shockley's solitary figure was some hundred yards ahead when, without warning, he pulled up sharply. Off to my left, Travis called out brusquely. 'Major, rein in *now!* Something's got him spooked.'

Complying immediately, I called back, 'What's wrong?

What has he seen?'

It was some time before the other man answered. 'Can't say. Maybe nothing. Could be just that dang nose of his.'

Ben and Davey reined in next to us and we all sat there speculating on what Shockley could possibly have discovered. That man remained atop his horse, still as a statue and seemingly oblivious to the passing of time. The fresh water was temptingly close and both teams began to whinny with impatience.

'How long do we leave him like this?' I demanded of the others.

Ben's reply was swift. 'Long as it takes, mister. Ain't ever known him to be wrong about something like this.'

Curbing my natural intolerance of delay, I dropped gratefully to the ground, to stretch my aching back. Yet no sooner had I done so than Davey hissed out, 'He's waving us forward, we gotta move.'

Cursing, I hurriedly clambered back onto the wagon and joined the others in a slow advance. At length we pulled up behind Shockley who, to my surprise, gave absolutely no acknowledgement of our presence. He just continued to sit his horse, whilst staring fixedly ahead. The man might as well have been in a trance and my annoyance was beginning to bubble over as I asked myself, How long must I accept this? I was, after all, supposedly in command.

Appearing almost eerily mindful of my thoughts, the ranger suddenly spoke. 'There, in the trees!'

The hairs rose up on the back of my neck as I replied, 'Who is it?'

Impatiently he responded, 'Someone or something is using those trees as cover!'

'I can't see a dang thing, Kirkham,' said Travis softly.

'Neither can I,' was that man's calm response, which left me utterly flabbergasted. But before I could protest he pivoted around in his saddle to face me. 'I don't have to see a snake in the grass to know it's there. It just is.'

There was something hypnotically compelling about his eyes that commanded my attention. But what was I to do about it? We couldn't wait out there all day. Fleetingly I wondered what Kirby would have done, only to push such thoughts from my mind. The decision was mine. Clambering off the wagon, I approached Shockley.

'Kirkham,' I called softly, so as not to alarm him.

There was no response, so this time I reached up and shook his arm. Pulling away as though I had just struck him, he wheeled his horse around so that he could directly face me.

'You just won't have it, will you? Because you can't see anything, it can't be there.'

I had had enough of this. Heatedly I said, 'If you're so damned sure, prove it. Ride on to the river and if nothing transpires we will all join you.'

The ranger stared at me for a full minute, eyes wild, as though in an opium induced haze. Then, with an almost imperceptible nod, he turned his mount back to the river. Rifle cocked at the ready, he inched forward, all the time scanning the tree line. No sooner had he left, than I was overcome by both unaccustomed indecision and guilt. That man knew the country and its people far better than I did. What if there was someone there, and I had just sent him to his death?

Clambering back onto my wagon, I joined Vicky and all the others in watching Shockley's slow progress. At any moment I expected a shot to ring out, but nothing at all happened and finally he reached the trees. Dismounting, he prowled around for some time before motioning for us to join him. With relief I urged the team forward. Within a matter of minutes all the horses were drinking from the wide, slow moving river. We had made it!

Shockley was still stalking about in the foliage, apparently unable to accept the outcome. Grim faced, the ranger tersely spat out a list of demands. 'We take the wagons over in relays, Travis first. The rest of us stand guard.' Turning to view Vicky, he almost snarled the question, 'You handled a long gun?'

Unbowed, she replied gamely, 'My pa done taught me, but it's been a long time.'

'That'll answer,' he returned, switching his unblinking gaze back to me. 'She can use the one you took off that soldier boy.'

Shockley was giving every appearance of usurping my position, but I was prepared to go along with him, as he so obviously knew his business. Complaining at his swiftly curtailed rest, Travis clambered reluctantly to his feet and headed for his wagon. The rest of us spread ourselves out along the riverbank, weapons cocked and ready. From the way that Vicky held her rifle, she obviously knew which end to point.

Stirring his unwilling team into action, Travis guided his wagon into the river. The water level was expected to be about chest high, and so it transpired. Any higher and the powder would have been at risk, as I did not have any great confidence in the water proofing of the barrels.

Slowly but surely he proceeded to the far side. Affected by Shockley's fears, we all expected a fusillade of shots at any moment, but none came. Yet the tension continued unabated, until I would almost have welcomed a burst of gunfire.

Finally the wagon emerged from the water, and came to a halt on the far bank. So now it was my turn. Hauling myself up and onto the seat, I grabbed the reins and we headed off down the bank. Once across, we would not have to traverse another river until we reached the Guadalupe.

As it slipped into the river our wagon tilted forward in an alarming fashion. My first such crossing had been a nerve-wracking experience, but I now felt myself to be an accomplished freighter. The water swirled about us, but remained just below the all-important cargo. Darting a glance at Vicky, I saw that she was taking her duties as guard seriously. Rifle at the ready, she carefully scanned the trees ahead.

The right hand lead horse stumbled and for a heart stopping moment I thought we were under attack, but then it recovered and maintained the pace. We were now halfway across. Travis bellowed out, 'Come on, Major, you're home and dry. Don't pay Kirkham any mind. He's all shit and no sugar!'

Then the left hand lead horse stumbled, only this time it didn't recover. Because a hole the size of a penny had just been punched in its neck. Whinnying with shock, it fell back on its haunches before slipping sideways under the water. Still in harness, it had the effect of dragging the others with it. Instinctively I pulled my knife, and leapt over the side. Suddenly immersed in cold water, I managed to keep my feet on the stony riverbed and yelled up to a very startled Vicky.

'When I cut the traces, get the other horses moving!'

Gunshots rang out as I powered towards the stricken horse. Blood stained the water, providing confirmation if any were needed that it had indeed been shot. Grasping the leather straps, I slashed at them with the well-honed blade. The instant that they were severed, I grabbed the bridle of the remaining lead animal. For the first time, I became aware of the shock of the chill water on my body. My boots felt leaden. My clothes clung to me. The remaining sovereigns, stitched into my jacket, acted as a dead weight.

From back in the trees I heard more shots and a choice selection of oaths. If there was any fighting to be done, I would be in serious trouble. Gradually we struggled through the gentle current, until I found myself looking directly up at Travis, standing before us on the bank. With his long rifle tucked tightly into his shoulder, he intently searched the opposing tree line for a target, but was not so occupied that he couldn't voice an opinion. 'That son of a bitch just doesn't give up, does he?'

'I wouldn't expect him to,' I retorted breathlessly. 'He's a British officer!'

With a titanic effort, I hauled my waterlogged form out of the river and heaved on the bridle. Urged on by Vicky and tugged forward by me, the unfortunate animals had little choice other than to drag their dripping burden out of the water.

Back across the river the tumult had died down. The three rangers were spread out along the bank, apparently unhurt. Uncomfortably aware of my sodden clothing, I shouted over, 'It was Speirs, wasn't it? Where is he now?'

Shockley's hard-edged voice answered, 'He was in the trees a ways down there. He's backed off some, but he's still local.'

'Damn the man,' I cursed to myself.

'We're coming over,' continued the ranger, 'so keep your eyes peeled.'

One at a time they rode across, whilst the rest of us stood guard. Having tethered his horse to a tree well back from the river, Shockley stalked towards me. Regarding me with a baleful expression, he said accusingly, 'You've brought some trouble down on our heads, ain't you? That ass boil knows how to shoot, and when to move.'

'If he's such a good shot, why'd he drill the horse and not you?' This came from a genuinely puzzled Davey.

To that at least I had the answer. 'I'm no use to him lying dead on some riverbed. Whatever he has been promised for apprehending me, is dependent on either producing me alive or irrefutable proof of my demise.'

It was Ben's turn to look puzzled. 'I don't understand the half of what you just said, or where he got another rifle from. I thought you ran him off with only that dang Pepperbox.' Then the awful implication of that hit him, and he cried out. 'Shit! That means he's kilt Frenchie *and* Kirby!'

Travis spat a wad of tobacco onto the ground as he exclaimed, 'Well, that just tears it!'

'So it stops here,' snarled Shockley.

Ignoring the others, Vicky flounced into our midst and jabbed a finger into my chest. 'If you don't get out of those wet duds, you won't be fit for stopping anything.'

Shivering violently, I could only agree. Looking pointedly at her I said, 'Perhaps you could fetch my blanket. I'm sure *you'll* recognize it.'

Some little time later I sat before a welcome fire, watching my clothes steam and pondering on Shockley's words. The man was right as usual. We would have to tackle Speirs before going any further. As it was, we could no longer proceed with Kirby's plan of splitting into two groups. We had insufficient horses to haul both wagons. And what of Kirby and his lone companion? Had Speirs really slaughtered them to obtain their weapons? I felt the colour flush into my face, as I considered the worst part of all this. That we were all in this god awful mess was, in large part, due to me.

I pulled myself up short. Recriminations of any kind were pointless. What I needed to do was find a way out and an idea was forming. Firstly, if we couldn't take both loads of powder with us, we would leave one. *Underground!* Bury all the barrels, and retrieve them later. Leave a wagon and hitch the spare horses to the other team for increased speed. That led me on to another scheme. Leaping to my feet, I strode over to confront Shockley. 'You and I are going to see this through to a conclusion together!'

He stared at me completely nonplussed, but I continued anyway. 'One wagon must remain here. Tonight, we will all bury its cargo.'

Ignoring the incredulous stares, I continued. 'Ben, Travis and you, Davey, will leave in darkness with the other wagon, our horses and Miss Fulsome. When daylight comes, or even before, Speirs will most surely come looking. He will find an apparently empty wagon, and an area of freshly turned earth.'

Shockley was regarding me with something akin to respect, whilst the others just appeared stunned. Travis was the first to voice his concern. 'It's madness! Where in tarnation will you be, when that bastard Speirs rides in?'

'Under the tarpaulin, on the wagon floor. With the sides in place, he'll have no chance to see me until it's too late. Then Kirkham and I share his horse and come after you.'

'Just like that,' exclaimed Travis sarcastically.

Before I could reply Shockley spoke out. 'You've got it all thought out, ain't you? And you know what? It could just work.' With that he just turned and walked away.

Taken completely aback, the other rangers could only accept his judgement, but it was obvious that they harboured some serious doubts.

Vicky's response came later when she joined me by the fire. 'You damn well better catch up with us.'

Reaching out to my steaming jacket, I took out three gold coins that I had recovered from Flaxton's body. With a smile, I placed them in the palm of her hand. 'Just in case.'

*

By the time darkness fell, my clothes were pretty much dry and thankfully so, as the fire had, of necessity, to be extinguished. With the unrelieved gloom came a feeling of depression. To my jaundiced eye even the trees lining both banks became menacing.

Both wagons were equipped with spades. With these we set to work excavating a trench to accommodate the powder barrels. With one man on watch and four digging, progress was swift, but back-breakingly gruelling. Although the sod was to be replaced, the excess earth was heaved into the river, enabling the cache of powder to be flush with the ground, and therefore well disguised to anyone more than a few yards away. Each spade load had to be carried there and soon my muscles were crying out for relief. Muffled curses, both Texan and English, flowed freely that night.

At last we were done. Earth had been packed over the barrels and the sod replaced. I hoped, for all our sakes, that they would not become infested with damp before we had the chance to recover them. That was always assuming that any of us made it back.

Glancing across the broad river to the tree line beyond, I wondered what Speirs had made of all our activity. It would undoubtedly draw him in once we had departed.

As I sat on the wagon bed, mopping sweat from my brow, Shockley padded up out of the gloom. 'How we gonna play this then, *General*?'

'When he is confident that we are gone, he will make directly for here. In this light he must know that *something* has taken place, but not what. I will be on this wagon bed, concealed under the tarpaulin with my shotgun. You can pick your own ground, as long as it is within sight of my position. Whatever happens he must not escape again, even if it means shooting his horse and leaving us afoot. Do you understand?'

'I ain't just come off the teat. I know what must be done, but I'll allow you got it all thought out.'

So it was all settled. I was to conceal myself, whilst the others led their horses past the wagon as cover. Shockley would mingle with them as they departed, dropping out at his pre-arranged spot.

With everything prepared, the others said their quiet farewells. Travis, Ben and Davey all accepted my hand, but there was no such formality with Vicky Fulsome. Pulling me tightly to her, so that I could feel the contours of her body, she said forcefully, 'Remember what I told you. Be sure and come back to us.'

CHAPTER NINE

I listened intently as the other wagon, with its attendant outriders, moved steadily away from the camp. The harsh reality of my plan rapidly became apparent, as I almost immediately felt a disconcerting remoteness from the outside world. Shockley had arranged the tarpaulin so that I could hear anyone approaching from the river, but I would be unable to see anything of relevance in any direction. The existence of side panels on the wagon meant that my vision was strictly limited to a small section of weathered timber. Such was the weight and thickness of the material laid over me that I began to imagine myself cocooned. With the strong odour of tar assaulting my nostrils, doubts crept in. I began to wonder if I had the necessary advantage over Speirs.

So total was the initial silence that I began to feel intimidated by it. But then, gradually, I was able to make out the sound of the river. The flow of water soothed my nerves, as I realized that if I could hear that, then I must surely be able to make out the approach of my nemesis. Unfortunately, this state of relative calm was not to last.

As time passed I found myself increasingly oppressed by the tarpaulin. My enclosed body began to overheat and I struggled with the onset of claustrophobia. It took all my willpower to remain perfectly still. Soon I was literally bathed in sweat and seriously concerned as to whether I would actually be able to react swiftly enough when the moment for action arrived.

To this day it is impossible for me to recall at what point I first heard a new sound emanating from the river. As it was I was suddenly aware that something had changed and all my niggling discomforts were forgotten, as I strained to discern just what it could be. Then it came to me. Something was struggling against the flow and it was undoubtedly a horse, as Speirs would desperately wish to keep his powder high and dry.

As the sound came closer, I longed to adjust my position to take a swift look, but of course that was out of the question. There was a brief disturbance as the rider urged his mount up onto the bank, before all returned to normal, with only the ripple of the water audible. Which meant that somewhere out there, Speirs was sitting in total silence, watching and waiting for any reaction to his presence.

As though in the throws of a fever, I felt a chill run up my spine, yet I continued to sweat heavily. I desperately longed to bellow out to Shockley, 'Shoot him, shoot him'. Yet the ranger would be situated beyond me and therefore even further away from the river. In the gloom he could not be certain of making the necessary kill shot, which he had to achieve if he were to bring our deadly game of cat and mouse to an end.

Then I heard a new sound. The creaking of leather. He was dismounting; responding to his suspicion of apparent normality in a way that had so far kept him alive. He would leave his horse and inch forward on foot, until entirely satisfied that all was as it should be. I could not help but admire the man, for all my fear and loathing of him. His soft footfalls drew nearer and the tension in my parboiled world became unbearable. Timing was everything. In the moment required to fling off the tarpaulin, he could quite easily place a ball in my head.

Then, so close that I could have reached out and touched it, something scrapped against the side of the wagon. Almost simultaneously, another totally unexpected noise made itself known; the sound of many horses approaching at a trot. A cocktail of fear and bafflement mingled fluidly together. The newcomers had obviously taken Speirs by surprise too, as he dropped to the ground, below and to the side of me. Frantically I tried to imagine who it could be.

The loud crack of a rifle split the air. It could only have been Shockley, so with that the time for pondering was over. Flinging the tarpaulin to one side, I took the shotgun in my left hand and vaulted out of the wagon. Landing in a crouched position on the opposite side to Speirs, I called across to him. 'I believe we're in more danger than you can imagine, Captain. Shoot me and you seal your own fate!'

Without waiting for his response, I twisted around, joyously aware of the cool refreshing breeze on my flesh. Amazingly the scene before me was exactly as I had envisaged it on hearing the rifle discharge. A large group of riders clad only in skins were milling around in total disarray. One of their number lay twitching on the ground and somewhere in that mêlée was Kirkham Shockley.

Pulling the butt tightly into my shoulder, I pointed the shotgun directly at them and bellowed out, 'Kirkham, drop for your life!'

The savages twisted towards me, struggling to identify this new threat emanating from the gloom. Pinpoint accuracy being irrelevant, I closed both eyes and squeezed the twin triggers. With an ear-splitting roar, both barrels spewed forth their deadly load. A mixture of lead balls and scrap metal scythed into the Comanches; which of course was, without any doubt, who they were.

Night vision still intact, I snapped open my eyes and watched as Shockley leapt to his feet and sprinted towards me. Two riderless horses galloped off into the night and with a collective howl of dismay the savages took fright and followed them.

Conscious of just who was behind me, I drew my revolver and did a rapid volte face. Directly opposite, but separated from us by the wagon, stood the tall menacing figure of Captain Speirs.

'I am constantly amazed by your resourcefulness, Major,' he remarked dryly and, under the circumstances, with notable composure. As if to emphasize his apparent mastery of the situation, the muzzle of his rifle was aimed unswervingly at my head, whereas the wagon's sides blocked my own weapon.

Aware that Shockley was beginning to ease his way around the front of the conveyance, I replied rapidly. 'Those Indians are confused and demoralized at present, but on realizing just how few of us there are, they will regroup and return. Your only chance of survival is to throw in your hand with us.'

My words carried the weight of conviction and had an effect on both men. Speirs, after brief consideration, nodded slowly and reluctantly lowered his rifle. In turn, Shockley ceased his cautious stalking and instead turned to address me. 'Those sons of bitches rode right over me. Left me no choice than to pop a cap.'

Speirs glanced dismissively at my companion, before directing his remarks at me. 'It appears that we should agree to a temporary truce, at least until we have seen off this heathen trash.' Inclining his head slightly towards Shockley he continued, 'What say you to that, my furtive colonial friend?'

Fixing his cold grey eyes on the captain's, Shockley replied, 'I aim to gut you like a fish, for what you did to my *compadres*! For now just remember who you're shooting at, when those varmints show up. And keep that god damn pistola out of my face. Savvy?'

Speirs's thin lips curled in the semblance of a smile that completely failed to reach his own eyes, before directing his next question at me. 'So, Major, what are your orders?' Although I could no longer claim rank in any army, men still waited on my instructions.

'Kirkham, you and the captain get a section of that sod up, whilst I reload this shotgun. I want two full-sized barrels placed out there to obstruct their approach, with powder trails leading back to this wagon. It's a profligate waste, but it may just save our skins. I take it that one of you possesses some Lucifers?'

Kirkham remained silent, so that it was left up to Speirs to drily reply. 'I am sure to have some amongst my meagre possessions.'

'Then let us make haste, gentlemen,' I urged, 'lest they catch us unprepared.'

In response to my urging, the two men ran over to the powder cache and swiftly removed some sections of sod. Our having retained only the one spade, Speirs accepted it without demure and dug down vigorously, whilst the ranger reloaded his rifle.

As there was only a light covering of earth, my fellow officer, for in reality that was what he was, soon recovered two of the concealed barrels. Having removed the wooden stoppers, both men then carried the containers some twenty yards out from the wagon, at a rough angle of forty-five degrees. The ensuing powder trail would act as the fuse.

Out in the darkness I could hear much commotion, as the Comanches built up their courage. Their guttural chanting had an unearthly quality, which set my nerves on edge. It made me uncomfortably aware of the massive disparity in numbers.

Having charged my shotgun, I propped it against a wagon wheel and then dragged the sheet of tarpaulin over to the trench. I wanted, at all costs, to avoid any of the savages discovering my concealed stock of powder, so I draped it over the freshly dug hole. Returning to the wagon, I found my two companions readying their own weapons as the hubbub reached a crescendo.

'Noisy buggers, aren't they, old boy?' Speirs's affected drawl was so evocative of my former life that I almost burst out laughing. I had to remind myself that he had been sent out to apprehend me at all costs. Taking up my shotgun, I glanced at the two powder trails.

'I'll thank you to produce those Lucifers now, Captain Speirs.'

'At your service, sir,' he replied with mock gallantry, at the same time pulling a small box from his trousers pocket. 'I seem to recall that you have used a version of this little ploy before, with some success.'

'It can't have been that good, mister,' snarled Shockley, 'else you'd be dead as a wagon tyre now.'

The infantry captain gave a wolfish grin as he responded to that. 'It would take a much better man than you to achieve that end.'

'If you don't both cease this now,' I interceded, 'we are all as good as dead!'

As if to support my words, there came the sudden pounding of many unshod hoofs. The Comanches were on the move. With the land still cloaked in gloom, I could only guess on when they would hit us. Our situation was truly desperate, but even so I was aware of Speirs's appraising look as he awaited my command. The man's coolness under duress was unnerving.

'The fuses, make ready,' I cried out. Both men knelt down next to their powder trail, Lucifers ignited and screened by their hands. 'The moment they detonate, we charge!'

The ground before us, which led away from the river, was flat and featureless. Once we had committed ourselves there would be nowhere to hide, or even defend. Everything would depend on timing and sheer aggression. From the inky blackness, the sound of thrumming hoofs grew nearer.

'*NOW!*'

Almost simultaneously the ground on either side of the wagon became visually alive as the powder ignited. The pyrotechnic display sped towards the waiting barrels, as all three of us grasped our weapons.

The hammering of the hoofs grew louder as the mass of warriors finally burst into view, alarmingly close to the powder barrels. Under the circumstances it was hard to gauge their numbers, but there had to have been in excess of two score.

With a grand boom, the barrel on the right flank exploded and night momentarily became day. From seemingly out of nowhere, both the blast and shards of wooden splinters struck horses and riders. The shock wave was dissipated by the open air, but was still strong enough to push their companions towards the second container.

'Stand fast,' I commanded somewhat unnecessarily, just as that charge also erupted. More animals crashed to the ground amidst a huge cloud of sulphurous smoke.

'Now,' I bellowed and as one, we leapt out from behind the wagon and raced forward. Screaming and shouting for effect, we covered the ground in seconds. The other two lagged behind slightly, so allowing me to discharge the scattergun safely. Directly before me, a dazed warrior was vainly attempting to gain control of his horse. The blast from my first discharge threw him backwards and into oblivion. Shoulder aching from the recoil, I fired the second load into a seething clutch of bronzed bodies and the resulting cloud of smoke instantly obscured them from me. The ensuing screams testified to my accuracy.

From off to my right, a lone Comanche staggered towards me, clutching a lance. A long splinter had bloodily skewered his belly, the unspeakable torment drawing his face into a mask of anguish. Hurling my heavy shotgun at him, I drew my revolver and thrust forward into the mêlée. On either side of me, my companions were firing aimed shots at every available target.

Advancing relentlessly, we fired into them at point blank range, quite literally powder burning our victims. To them we must have seemed like death dealing apparitions, but our vicious progress hid a desperate vulnerability. I possessed one Paterson Colt with five chambers, whilst Shockley had two of the same. Speirs had his six shot Pepperbox. Once they were discharged there would be no opportunity to reload. We would then be left with two rifles between us and our hunting knives.

Then calamity struck. Speirs cried out in alarm, 'It's jammed,' and thrusting the Pepperbox into his belt, he swung out wildly with his rifle at the two warriors confronting him. Veering off towards him, I levelled my revolver directly at the nearest man's head and squeezed the trigger. The weapon bucked in my hand. Through the resultant flash and smoke plume, I glimpsed blood and brains gushing from the exit wound. Speirs had meanwhile managed to slam the rifle stock into his other opponent's ribs. With a grunt of pain, that man collapsed to his knees, totally unable to fend off the soldier's *coup de grâce*. With unconcealed satisfaction, Speirs brought the butt down onto the back of his head, shouting over to me as he did so, 'My thanks to you, sir.'

Flushed with the excitement of fighting a common foe, I again had to remind myself that we were in fact deadly enemies, honouring a truce solely out of necessity. From my left there came the comforting report and powder flash of a Colt discharging, indicating that Shockley was holding his own. The smoke and dust generated by the twin explosions had by now completely dissipated and there was only the gloom of night to disguise our paltry numbers. Before me a powerfully built mounted warrior was shouting out commands. He could not be allowed to re-establish order amongst the war band.

With only two chambers remaining, I had to think fast. Cocking my weapon, I charged towards him. Another mounted warrior thrust his horse towards me, using only his legs to control it. Notching an arrow to his bow, he took swift aim. Instinctively I swung my revolver up and fired directly into his chest. With an anguished cry he tumbled backwards, disappearing from view.

One chamber left.

Maintaining momentum, I reached the Comanche leader and powered myself off the ground. Catching him side on, I managed to wrap my left arm tightly around his torso. The horse stumbled slightly, but remained upright. Without giving him time to react, I smashed the frame of my revolver into his face, and then rammed the muzzle under his chin. For a fleeting moment I saw the horror registering on his battered and bloodied face, as the savage realized with dreadful certainty that he was about to die. Turning my face away, I squeezed the trigger. With a roar the final chamber discharged, sending the .36 calibre ball up into his brain, before exiting through the roof of his skull in a shower of red and grey slime. Drops of blood spattered on my face, as his lifeless legs released their grip and we both fell heavily to the ground. Landing on my back, all the breath was knocked out of me and I lay there winded and completely helpless.

The bloodied corpse lay across my upper body, severely hampering my efforts to draw air into my lungs. As I attempted to heave him off, I was aware of a coating of grease, which made my task all the more difficult. Frantically bucking under him, I finally managed to roll the Comanche away. Greedily sucking in air, I was aware that the sounds of battle seemed to have diminished. Individual riders were galloping away as though demoralized by the sudden death of their leader. It was well known amongst the rangers, that any apparent change of fortune was often sufficient to persuade the savages to break off an engagement, even if in reality they had the upper hand.

Even though still dazed, I felt a tremendous surge of relief flow through me. Had three men really managed to drive off a whole war band at least ten times their number? Feeling strength returning, I searched around for my revolver, only to jump with shock as a horse suddenly thundered up to me. Gazing up at its rider in disbelief, I witnessed his triumphant expression, as he levelled a fully extended bow at my defenceless form.

In the instant that he loosed the arrow, a single shot rang out. A shattering pain engulfed my left arm, but even through that I was aware that my attacker was no longer in sight. Although still on my back, I could easily make out the wooden shaft attached to the iron headed arrow embedded in my upper arm. My head swam and I struggled to focus. Then I heard Shockley's voice as he ran towards me. Unusually for him he sounded almost jubilant.

'God damn it, Major. We did it. *You* did it. I ain't never seen the like before, nor ever will again.'

Fighting against the agony coursing through my body, I looked directly at the normally grim faced ranger and favoured him with a smile. I was gratified, in a way that transcended the pain, to see it returned with genuine warmth and admiration. Due to this uncharacteristic pre-occupation, Shockley failed to catch the movement nearby.

Captain Speirs emerged from out of the gloom and positioned himself behind and to the side of the euphoric frontiersman.

'What a touching little scene,' he remarked dryly, as he placed the multiple barrelled, supposedly jammed Pepperbox Pistol to the side of Shockley's skull and squeezed the trigger. As the upper barrel erupted, the ranger's head jerked forward like that of a marionette. I could only watch in horror as his temple disintegrated in a welter of blood and brain matter. So close had the muzzle been on discharge, that the man's hair was smouldering from the powder flash. Bizarrely the smile remained fixed in place, as Ranger Shockley's now lifeless body slumped to the ground.

With a supreme effort I managed to get to my feet, but the world around me began to drift again. Totally incapable of saving myself I fell back, and then down. Again the air vacated my lungs, but this time I was aware only of a strange blackness enveloping me as all sensation left me and I surrendered to the void.

CHAPTER TEN

My eyes flicked open, accepting far more light than I could possibly deal with. Snapping them shut again, I resolved to take things slowly. My heart was racing, so I began drawing in deep draughts of air. That had the effect of steadying me, but failed to dispel the appalling ache in my left arm. To compound matters my legs felt strangely constricted, so I attempted some movement to relieve them. No amount of effort could achieve that, so I risked opening my eyes again. What I saw overrode the discomfort and chilled me to the core. My legs were bound together at the ankles by a strip of rawhide, which in turn was tied to a short wooden post hammered into the earth.

'This cannot be,' I half muttered to myself. Twisting around I began to take in my surroundings. I was back at the camp by the river. The major source of my discomfort, the Comanche arrow, remained embedded in my arm. Granted it was only a flesh wound, but the pain was excruciating. And then everything flooded back; the desperate battle with the war party, my injury, Kirkham Shockley's horrific death, and *Speirs*!

'Well, well, so the hero of the hour is awake.'

Jerking to the right, I saw the speaker lounging casually against the side of my wagon. As I watched, he pushed

98

himself upright and sauntered towards me.

'You bastard,' I cried out. 'There was no need to slaughter that man, he had done you no ill!'

'The pain from your wound has obviously addled your quite considerable wits. That colonial was a born killer. He would have carried out his threat to me at the first opportunity. As it was I had a stroke of luck.' By way of explanation of that last remark, the captain none too gently prodded my left arm with his boot. Daggers of sheer torment launched themselves through my body as I twisted away from him.

There was a look of anticipation on his face as he observed my suffering. 'One thing you should be aware of, Major Collins, I am an officer to be sure, but definitely no gentleman!'

As the full import of his words hit me, the raging anger subsided. The figure looming over me was quite definitely the most dangerous individual that I had yet encountered. Blind rage was always more dangerous to the person displaying it and indulging in it with this man would surely kill me. Taking a deep breath, I settled back on the ground and appraised my captor.

'Perhaps it would benefit us both if you made your intentions known, Captain Speirs.'

The other man gave a mirthless laugh before replying. 'My *intention* is to die a man of wealth and position. When I have relieved you of the sovereigns stitched into your jacket I will have some of the former. Delivering you alive to the British *chargé d'affaires* in Washington on the Brazos will help me on my way to the latter. But first I will need to remove that arrow before infection sets in. It should serve to keep you breathing *and* will assist me in removing said jacket.' With that he turned away and stalked off towards the river.

I have no idea how much time passed before he returned to me. The throbbing in my arm never ceased, and the severity of the binding on my ankles was causing me some cruel discomfort. For a brief time at least, I either passed out or fell into a fitful sleep. I came to with a start shortly before his return. Giving me a cursory glance, the tall officer dropped some kindling and swiftly constructed a small fire.

'It occurs to me that your wound, once cleaned, may need cauterizing. I'm sure you're familiar with the technique.'

I winced from a combination of pain, alarm and surprise. Surely he hadn't witnessed the whole episode with Kirby.

Trying desperately to think logically I asked, 'What became of my two companions? I know that you have their firearms.'

Speirs appeared bored by the subject, but nonetheless condescended to reply. 'If you look over by the river, you will observe the horse that is to carry you to Washington.'

I did as instructed and was shocked by what I saw. Ground tethered and grazing peacefully was Frenchie's short brown Quarter Horse. 'So you killed him too,' I stated sadly.

It was a statement rather than a question, but the captain shrugged his shoulders and responded anyway. 'I came upon him looting the body of my sergeant, so I could hardly let him live. As for the other fellow, you'd already had your entertainment with him, so I left him where he lay. He lives or dies. It's of no account to me.'

With that he placed my hunting knife into the fire. Then, from inside his jacket, he produced a length of rawhide. Seizing my right arm, he looped it around my wrist, tied it off and then stretched it out behind my head. Unbeknown to me he had already hammered a second stake into the ground. Within a matter of seconds the only limb that I could move was my left arm, but of course he had plans for that.

Removing his jacket, he rolled up the sleeves of his blood spattered white shirt. Catching my glance, he obviously realized that I was scrutinizing his appearance, because anger flared in his eyes.

'The next blood stains on this shirt will be yours!'

So saying and without any warning, he grabbed the arrow shaft with both hands, and savagely snapped it in two. I had known that it had to be done, to facilitate the extraction, but nothing had prepared me for the ensuing pain. My whole body went rigid with shock and rivers of sweat began to pour from me. A sense of anger and outrage exploded within me and I struggled wildly against the rawhide straps.

'Come now, Major,' muttered Speirs mildly, as though gently rebuking a child. 'We're just getting started. This arrow has been cunningly barbed to prevent it being withdrawn. The only way to extract it is to force it forward and out.'

There was an edge of excitement to his voice that spoke volumes and for the first time I felt real despair. I was quite obviously in the hands of a sadistic madman. My captor only had to return me alive, whilst any ill treatment inflicted on me could be explained away as a medical necessity, following my conflict with the Comanches.

Approximately six inches of wooden shaft protruding from my upper arm remained. The metal head had obviously struck at an angle, but not broken the bone. Standing astride me, he dropped to his knees and then settled himself onto my lower torso. I immediately felt my breathing restricted and was uncomfortably aware that I was now completely immobile. Catching my desperate glance, Speirs licked his lips before speaking.

'This procedure will cause you great pain. I need to be in control at all times.'

As he said this I noticed that, as though compensating for my own reaction, his rate of breathing had increased and a thin sheen of sweat now covered his forehead. The man was actually revelling in the anticipation of what was to follow.

I twisted and strained with all my strength, but it was to no avail. Bound hand and foot, with his body weight bearing down on me, I was his to mistreat as he wished. Leaning to his right, he took hold of my injured arm and twisted it, so as to access the flesh opposite the penetration point. Grasping his own knife, he placed the razor sharp tip onto my pale skin and pressed in, then down. My stomach tightened, my legs began to tremble violently and I howled out in pain. I truly believed that he was trying to amputate my arm. Pulling his bloody knife back, he remained astride me, blatantly savouring my suffering as I writhed beneath him. With my breathing severely constricted, I was unable to sustain my reaction for long. As the tears in my eyes cleared, I realized that he was talking to me.

'That incision will enable me to push the head past the bone and out.'

Seizing my arm with his right hand, he placed the palm of his left onto the broken end of the shaft and began to push. I could never have envisaged that such pain could be both possible and sustainable. The arrowhead began to tear through virgin flesh, sending vicious bursts of agony lancing through my whole body. I could not withstand it and yet had no option. The screams no longer seemed to emanate from me, they just existed.

How long I endured it for I will never know, but it did finally end. Without warning the pressure just ceased, to be replaced by an all-consuming ache. As my resistance subsided, the captain opened his eyes and rocked back onto his heels. There was a look of twisted pleasure etched onto his face. At that point I slipped into a state of blessed unconsciousness.

When I came to, the sun was going down. My three limbs remained bound, so I lay there perfectly still for some time, not wishing to attract Speirs's attention. Finally I slowly turned my head to scrutinize the expected wreckage of my arm. It was with some surprise that I found it to be efficiently bandaged with the detached sleeve of my once white shirt. There was a strong smell of alcohol, which suggested that my captor had poured whiskey over the wound rather than cauterized it. Perhaps there had not been any pleasure to be gained from that procedure once I had passed out.

My hesitant movement had registered with Speirs and he drifted back from the river with a water canteen. Without any preamble he remarked, 'We will remain here for the night so that you may rest. At first light we depart for the Brazos River.'

He had made no reference to the ordeal that he had subjected me to and anger bubbled up within me. 'I could have you cashiered for what you did today,' I accused him coldly.

Strangely subdued, Speirs avoided my eyes as he answered. 'You're alive, aren't you? It was necessary. Besides, who would believe the word of a deserter against that of a serving officer?'

I wanted to rail against him for the brutality of his

actions, but fought against it. I was completely in his power and he knew it. Changing tack I asked, 'Are you not curious as to why I remained in Texas?'

Finally fixing his eyes on me, he sneered. 'A comely wench and a pouch full of sovereigns will turn any man's head. Beyond that I don't really care. My only concern is that you survive to reach captivity. When I bring you in, the name of Hugo Speirs will finally count for something. Enough talk. Sleep while you can, for tomorrow we will be covering a lot of distance.'

The next day began in the same way as the previous period had ended. Painfully! The ever-present ache was sufficiently severe to test my sanity, but at least I was still alive. *And* I had finally slept a little.

There was movement from over by the river and I watched carefully as the captain strode towards me. There was something about his demeanour that struck a chord of recognition within me. The man was uneasy, but working hard to conceal it. Since I couldn't possibly be the cause of his disquiet, there had to be something else. As he approached me, I made another observation. He had my Colt Revolver tucked into his belt along with his own Pepperbox. It was to be expected, but it still rankled.

' 'Tis an impressive piece, Major,' he commented, supplying proof, if indeed it was required, that he didn't miss a thing. Silently he knelt down and sliced through the cord securing my right arm. With the welcome freedom came yet more pain, as the circulation returned. Dropping a water canteen and some beef jerky in my lap, he then turned and walked away.

'Something's troubling you, Captain,' I called after him. 'If it concerns the savages, you'd best tell me.'

The man stopped, as though about to speak, then

apparently thought better of it and continued back to where the horses were grazing by the riverbank. He was obviously preparing for our departure.

I sat up too quickly, so that my head swam. Fighting the sensation, I gulped down some cool water, which immediately made me feel better. Encouraged, I followed it by taking a bite out of the jerky. Chewing on the strongly flavoured meat, I took the opportunity to view my surroundings. What I saw sent yet another shudder through my body.

The tarpaulin had been heaved clear of the powder store. A keg, with its stopper missing, had been placed at the edge of the partially covered trench and had a long powder trail running from it. Speirs obviously intended to blow up the magazine.

Within minutes he was back, leading both horses and this time there was no disguising the agitation that he felt. Looking down at me, his eyes met mine and he could contain himself no longer.

'Something is amiss,' he muttered. 'Can you not feel it? We are no longer alone.'

Sensing a slight shift in the balance of power, I was in no mood to soothe him. Instead I replied cuttingly, 'The only thing I can feel is pain sinking its talons into me. If you genuinely consider that we are under threat, cut me loose this instant *and* arm me!'

'Go to hell!'

'If your suspicions are correct you may get there before me.'

At that his face flushed livid and I was sure that he would strike me. Instead he drew his knife and sliced through the rawhide around my ankles. Rolling to my right, I ended up on my hands and knees, where I remained, desperately trying to control the nausea that had suddenly overwhelmed me. Then I heard an ominous double click, as my own revolver was brought to full cock.

'If you attempt to mount before I say, I will place a ball in one of your limbs. Be assured it will *not* kill you until *after* we reach Washington!'

Giving up any attempt to stand, I instead assumed a sitting position from where I could observe his movements. My earlier fears were confirmed, as he moved directly to the end of the powder trail some few yards away. He really did intend to destroy all my gunpowder. Looking desperately around for a weapon, *any weapon*, I noticed my shotgun temporarily secured to his saddle with rawhide. I contemplated making a dash for it, before cursing myself for a fool. In my condition he would cut me down before I laid a hand on it. I watched helplessly as he placed my revolver in the crook of his arm, to enable him to ignite a Lucifer. As it flared into life he turned to face me. Standing there, apparently all-powerful, with the flaming Lucifer in his left hand and my Colt in his right, his thin lips twisted into a sardonic smile. One thing was for certain: *at that moment Captain Hugo Speirs was afraid of nothing in this world!*

The lead ball caught him in the left shoulder, causing him to pirouette like a ballet dancer. The shock of the smashing blow created two separate events. His right forefinger contracted, discharging my own revolver harmlessly into the air. Far more seriously he abruptly lost control of his left hand and the burning Lucifer dropped to the ground. The marksman appeared to be hidden in the undergrowth some distance away, but on our side of the Colorado River.

Knowing that he could not coerce me onto a horse whilst both under fire and injured, Speirs thrust my weapon into his belt, gratuitously nudged the Lucifer into the powder trail, and then ran for his mount. The sudden change of position saved him from the next ball, which kicked up earth just beyond the spot where he had been standing. I watched in absolute horror, as the powder trail flared into vigorous life. Whoever was concealed in the trees would have no chance of reaching it in time if indeed they even chose to, so it was left to me. As Speirs heaved himself awkwardly into his saddle, I lurched to my feet and staggered towards the weaving cloud of sulphurous smoke. The speed with which the grains ignited was truly frightening. If the conflagration reached the keg before I did, Speirs's quest would finally be over along with his chances of advancement, as there would be little to prove that I had ever existed.

To the sound of drumming hoofs, I forced my aching body into the semblance of a run. I was hideously aware that I only had the one chance. With only a few feet to go, I literally threw myself forward. My already bruised chest landed squarely on the flaring powder, but that action in itself was not sufficient. In bygone times its ability to burn in a confined space was seen by many as magical. Thrusting my arms out, I grasped the keg and turned it on its side, the uncorked hole pointing safely skywards. Then, by thrashing madly about like a stranded fish, I scattered the remaining powder trail amongst the grass.

Rolling carefully to my right, I lay back quite exhausted. From the direction of the river I heard slow, laboured footsteps as my mysterious saviour approached. Unarmed and almost fearful of whom it could be, I raised myself onto one elbow and gazed towards the trees. The sight that greeted my eyes rendered me stunned, and left me gawping like an idiot.

CHAPTER ELEVEN

'You look like you done seen a ghost,' croaked the apparition before me.

I watched in utter disbelief as the Texas Ranger known as Sergeant Kirby crept slowly towards me. Deathly pale, he appeared to have aged some twenty years. Dried blood was caked to his neck just below the jaw line. His shoulders were stooped and he sucked air in as though every breath was his last, but there was no doubting his ability with the revolver that he clutched tightly in his right hand.

He maintained his painfully slow progress until almost colliding with me. Peering down at me, his red-rimmed eyes locked onto mine. 'What the hell was all that squirming about? You turned into a reptile or what?'

That he still had his wits about him could not be disputed. I felt a strong urge to hug him, but instead contented myself by grinning broadly as I struggled to my feet once more. Breathlessly I explained to him about the buried powder store and of the desperate battle with the Comanches ending in Shockley's death. As I touched on the subject of my own ordeal he slowly shook his head.

'I done heard it all and saw some of it.'

I stared at him in amazement. 'You mean to say that you witnessed the whole thing?'

He nodded defiantly before replying, 'You hollered fit to wake snakes. I used the whole ruckus as cover to ford the river. Never got chance of a clear shot and I ain't much for running right now.'

Taken aback, I swayed slightly and he reached out with his left hand to steady me. 'You'd better sit back down before you fall.'

Gratefully, I dropped to the ground. Transfixing my gaze, Kirby spoke with a controlled ferocity. 'That cockchafer's got nine lives, but he made his mistake by not claiming mine.'

I expressed my own opinion on that. 'I believe he enjoyed the thought of leaving you to suffer alone.'

He emitted a strange croak, which I took to be a laugh. 'Only now I got a pardner. Excepting we're both whipped, with only one belt gun between us. I swear that bastard Englishman's gonna answer for this.' He looked away and then back at me, as though something had just occurred to him. 'No offence.'

I patted him gently on the arm. 'None taken!'

For some time we just sat in companionable silence, both of us content merely to exist without effort. Then the absence of any threat and the gentle ripple of the river lulled us both into an exhausted sleep. It was late afternoon before I awoke, to find Kirby snoring noisily beside me and thankfully everything else as we had left it. My arm was aching abominably and there were spots of blood on the makeshift bandage. Hunger gnawed on me like a prairie dog and I determined to light a fire regardless of risk. We both needed hot food if we were to recover. Having slowly collected some kindling, I built a small fire on the same spot that Speirs had used. The very thought of his name made me stiffen with anger, but this reaction was swiftly followed by concern. For I knew that, even wounded and in shock, he had deliberately chosen the direction of his flight.

Ranger Kirby jerked awake to the mouth-watering smell of hot pinto beans, tortillas and scalding coffee. Our diet on the trail rarely varied, but to us that meal was little short of a banquet. For some time we devoted ourselves solely to gorging, now and again coming up for air, before returning to the trough.

Finally we were done and with an enormous belch, Kirby staggered to his feet and hoarsely announced, 'I'm gonna take a shit, then we need to jaw a spell.'

I smiled and nodded. He was, as ever, graphically direct in his speech. Watching him stumble off into the trees, I felt tremendous warmth for the man.

Upon his return we sat before the dying fire, nursing mugs of coffee and almost contentedly watched the sun go down. As I had knowledge of the others, it was left to me to spoil the mood. 'He's gone after them knowing that I will have to follow him. You realize that, don't you?'

'Because of Vicky?'

'Yes,' I replied. 'He does not know of my connection with her, but he will know that I could not leave a woman to his tender mercies.'

I briefly related to him the events that led to the four of them setting out alone. He listened intently before stating, 'That fella just don't give up. If you'd had more like him, the British would still be running this continent.'

'I just hate to think what that bastard could do to Vicky if he gets his hands on her.'

'She's with three rangers and he's wounded. That's got to count for something.'

And there we left it. No amount of discussion could alter

the fact that the captain had a good start on us, which therefore afforded him the first move.

My last night by the Colorado River was one of complete tranquillity. We took the considered decision not to mount a guard, so as to obtain the maximum amount of sleep. Kirby was of the opinion that following such a disastrous reversal of fortune, the Comanches were highly unlikely to return to such an ill fated spot.

Upon awakening the next morning I actually felt glad to be alive. My companion was already up and about. A small fire was crackling away and I could smell coffee, or at least what passed for it on the frontier.

'You would make somebody a good wife, my friend,' I suggested playfully.

'Keep running your mouth off like that and you won't see yours again.'

A short while later, our belongings stowed away, we rode slowly through the battlefield. I was mounted on Frenchie's Quarter Horse, which not having suffered a rider for many days was truly fresh and skittish. The sights and smells around us also quite possibly affected it. It was the first time that I had seen the carnage in daylight and the experience was truly unpleasant. The Comanche dead had suffered a variety of wounds: gunshot, splinter, blast and burns, all of which imparted their own characteristics. The bodies were beginning to turn, so that the smell drifting up from them was truly stomach churning.

The most dreadful sight was undoubtedly that of Kirkham Shockley. He lay where he had fallen, his skull almost destroyed by the point blank penetration. It pained us both to leave him that way, but we needed to conserve our strength for the pursuit ahead. His burial would have to wait for whichever party returned to recover the stash of powder.

Our purpose was the recovery of any useable firearm to offset our severe lack of them. Only one weapon appeared suitable and I almost missed that. A .50 calibre smooth bore musket jutted out from beneath a bloodied torso. Dismounting to extract it, I cried out with delight upon discovering that it had a percussion mechanism. Reluctantly dragging the greasy corpse onto its back, I located a pouch containing an assortment of lead balls and percussion caps, which really lifted my spirits. At least now I was no longer completely defenceless.

And so, finally, we left the Colorado River behind. For the sake of our sanity we dared not contemplate what might be happening ahead of us. For now it was sufficient that we were on the move once more.

For the rest of that day we maintained a steady and almost continuous pace, stopping only to stretch our aching muscles and relieve ourselves as required. I had fashioned a rudimentary sling for my left arm, which helped reduce the level of throbbing. My body was also benefiting from the lack of weight that it had to support, which was the only favourable outcome from the theft of my gold sovereigns.

For most of the time we maintained a companionable silence, content to concentrate on our surroundings as we passed rapidly through the countryside. Occasionally I caught sight of the grim, determined expression on Kirby's face and realized that it probably mirrored my own. We were two men most definitely set on revenge.

Travis's party had a full two-day start on us, plus any distance they had covered that first night. As the sun began to slip over the horizon again we debated whether to push on through the night, but decided against it. Both of us, still

suffering from the effects of our respective ordeals, pre-
ferred to opt for a full night's sleep. Since we had no idea
of anybody else's position, we definitely had to settle for a
cold camp. Beef jerky and biscuits washed down with river
water formed our evening meal. Then, without more ado,
we both curled up in our blankets, again gambling that we
would not be discovered, and so slept the night away.

As the sun began its lazy arc into the sky, we two convales-
cents awoke almost simultaneously. As normal after an
unguarded night, we both lay there without moving whilst
adjusting to the sights and sounds around us. The horses
were still grazing peacefully, which was always a sure sign
that all was well.

Rubbing his teeth with a none too clean forefinger,
Kirby regarded me steadily. 'With the weight on that wagon
we'll catch up with them today and no mistake.'

'I don't doubt that, but where do you think Speirs will
be?'

Kirby's reply was scathing. 'That pus weasel will be
sneaking around waiting for an opening. He'll expect us to
be following, so he'll stay on the flanks and with these
shooting irons, there's not a damn thing we can do about
it.'

He was right of course. With a rifle, shotgun and two
repeaters, Speirs had us completely outmatched. All we
could hope to do initially was join up with the others and
alert them to the danger. Well rested after a long night's
sleep, we were both anxious to be off. Tellingly, Kirby was
now able to heave his own saddle up onto his mount whilst
I, the one-armed man, still required assistance. Just as I
finally settled myself onto the back of the Quarter Horse, I
was struck by a thought of such gravitas that I almost cried
out.

We both knew that Speirs's target would probably be Vicky, but what if, under extreme duress, she in turn disclosed my relationship with her cousin? That didn't bear thinking about. I undoubtedly knew what Hugo Speirs was capable of better than anyone. That fact alone meant that had I been unaccompanied, I would almost certainly have ridden my new mount to death.

On and on we cantered across the prairie, the lush subtropical vegetation now just a distant memory. Noon came and went. I was beginning to despair that we would ever catch up with them, when Kirby reined in abruptly. He had just crested a rise, so I urged my horse forward to join him.

A burst of pure joy surged through me. Before us was the wagon with its two outriders. I had survived to rejoin them after all. On the point of galloping down to meet them, I glanced at Kirby and noticed that he wore a puzzled expression.

'Something ain't right down there. There's only three of them and they're a horse short!'

Finally taking time to scrutinize the little group carefully, I realized to my horror that he was right. 'Vicky! It's Vicky that's missing. Oh my god, that bastard's got her!'

The recognition that we had arrived too late was almost too much to accept. Spurring my mount down the slope, I raced off towards the rangers, oblivious of my own safety and the fact that I only had one good arm. My reckless approach had them levelling their weapons, until they recognized I was friend rather than foe. Their universal smiles of welcome turned to expressions of sheer amazement when they saw who it was that followed me in.

'God damn, but you made it, Major,' bellowed out a genuinely overjoyed Travis. 'And look who you brought with you.' Pointing directly at my companion he continued, 'I thought you was dead for sure, you old bull turd!'

'Well, I ain't, you old coot,' Kirby replied flatly. 'But Kirkham's paroled to Jesus and there ain't no bringing him back.'

Shock registered on the faces of all three rangers. Of those that had left San Antonio, Shockley had seemed the least likely to succumb.

Dismounting, I could contain myself no longer. 'Vicky, where is she? Surely you didn't allow her to wander off alone?'

Both Ben and Davey looked a little sheepish, but Travis remained characteristically defiant. 'She had to take a shit and you know what women are like. Can't do it with a bunch of fellas gawking at them. Now if we'd offered to watch her taking a poke, well I wager that would've been diff—'

Abruptly cutting him off, I railed at him, 'So you just let her ride off out of sight, with a maniac like Speirs on the loose.'

That argument failed to make any impression on the grizzled ranger. 'You see any of us wearing dresses? What else were we to do? And you were supposed to have kilt that poxy English son of a bitch.'

This was getting me nowhere, so rounding on Kirby I said, 'We've got to find her!'

To his credit that man had the good grace to appear uncomfortable, but he emphatically shook his head.

'No dice, Thomas.' Out of the corner of my eye I was aware that the unaccustomed use of my Christian name had registered with the others. 'My orders are to get this powder back to Béxar County. That comes before anything else. You should understand that, fella, you paid for all of this!'

'Some things count for more than money,' I replied heatedly.

'That's why we gotta get this load back,' countered Kirby. 'It's likely enough hundreds of folks will suffer at the hands of those heathen savages if we don't.'

The man was not for turning. All I could do was push for one consideration. 'At least give me your revolver. I stand little or no chance against Speirs with just this musket.'

The two of us stood almost face to face and I was determined not to back down. Our eyes remained locked for many seconds, before he finally broke the tension. With a wry smile he stated, 'Yeah well, I suppose I can stand to do that. Just don't lose it. You've been getting a mite careless with weapons of late.'

With a measure of satisfaction, I accepted the proffered belt gun and then handed him my percussion musket. Without more ado, I tucked the Colt into my belt and grabbed the reins.

'How long since she left?'

'I ain't never had no watch, Major,' said Travis laconically. 'But she should have been back well before you arrived. She wandered off over yonder apiece.'

Hauling myself one handed into the saddle, I wheeled off in the pointed direction.

It was but a short canter to the crest of the next rise. Dismounting, I could still see the wagon with its four rangers quite clearly. I had no idea what awaited me over the ridge, but knowing whom I was up against I could not afford to leave anything to chance. Dropping the reins, I first walked then crawled awkwardly to the rim, where I removed my slouch hat before looking tentatively over. A swift glance revealed only empty undulating terrain without a soul in sight. Had he taken her with him, or was he waiting beyond the next brow for me to come looking? Another third alternative didn't bear thinking about, so I decided to assume that he was waiting to line me up in his sights. Therefore I would have to take the long way around.

Carefully backing off down the slope, I inelegantly mounted up and headed off around the right flank. My inclination was to ride like the wind, but I had to temper it with caution. Having lost sight of the wagon, I gradually wended my way around to where I presumed him to be. Taking my bearings, I estimated that I must be some 135 degrees around the semi-circle that I was travelling, and despite the mild weather I felt a chill descend on me.

Trusting my senses, I slid from the saddle and there being nowhere to tether it, hobbled the animal's front legs with a strip of rawhide. Everything seemed to take so much longer with only the one good arm. Drawing Kirby's revolver from my belt, I carefully pulled the hammer back to full cock before advancing, mindful of the fact that Speirs would be attuned to the slightest noise.

The ground that I would have been expected to travel over was off to my left, beyond another rise. I was praying that his eyes would be glued to that, whilst I came around and below him on his left flank. The tension in my body mounted as I inched forward, terrifyingly aware of the array of weapons in his arsenal. If he had discovered my approach, Speirs could have dropped me from two hundred yards before I even clapped eyes on him.

Gradually I advanced, my eyes roaming over the landscape as I desperately sought out my prey. Then my heart literally lurched, as I suddenly made out a prone human form on the ground, off to my right and certainly not where I had expected to see anyone. Fighting the temptation to rush forward, I gradually angled over there, all the time searching for the expected threat. As I got closer I recognized Vicky's burgundy coloured dress and I felt a wave of relief at having found her. But that was immediately tempered by doubt. Why was she not moving?

As my eyes swivelled frantically between her and the surrounding terrain, I instinctively knew that something was badly wrong. Throwing all caution to the wind, I rushed forward and knelt down beside her. Bracing myself for the expected hammer blow of a rifle ball striking me, I gazed at Vicky's recumbent figure. The dress hugged her form as finely as ever, but as long as I live I will never forget her face. The pale unblemished skin had been replaced with a blotchy complexion the colour of beetroot. The eyes were bulging, whilst her swollen tongue protruded beyond her mouth in a truly ghastly fashion. Sweeping aside the lace attached to her collar caused my blood to run cold. A length of wet rawhide cord had been placed around her neck and then knotted tightly. The warmth from her flesh and the mild breeze had combined to slowly dry it out, so that it had inexorably choked her to death. Anger and shame welled up inside of me. Was there no limit to that man's capacity for evil deeds?

It appeared that he possessed not an ounce of human feeling or compassion. And yet I had brought all this down on her, along with all the others. Finding her in that condition left me totally bereft and so it was almost absentmindedly that I unsheathed my hunting knife. Ignoring the pain, I slipped my left arm out of its sling and using thumb and forefinger, took hold of the knot wedged against her neck. Gingerly I forced the point inside the band of rawhide. Even though she had expired, I was oddly fearful of drawing blood from her once beautiful features. The still glorious dark hair framed her now hideous complexion, as I sliced the blade outwards.

The rawhide fell away from her neck, leaving a vivid mark where it had throttled her. Sickened, I sheathed the knife and then belatedly recollecting my circumstances I glanced swiftly around. All was peaceful, but that didn't necessarily mean anything.

Then I heard it! Or maybe only even sensed it. Perhaps it was just the wishful imagination of a desperately unhappy man. Trembling slightly I turned back to Vicky, and stared intently at her bloated features. Again there was an almost ethereal whisper. This could not be, she was trying to communicate! Dropping down, I pressed my right ear to her mouth and listened intently. Nothing, nothing at all. This was madness. The woman was dead, for God's sake! Yet then it came again. Almost non-existent. I only understood it because I recognized it.

'*Sarah!*'

Scrabbling to my feet, I bolted back to my horse, oblivious of anything else around me. If she could talk, then she had to be alive! Grabbing my water canteen, I retraced my steps with a speed that I hadn't believed myself capable of. Flinging myself down next to her, painfully jarring my arm in the process, I pressed the mouth of the container to her lips. The life-giving water trickled out . . . only to run off her face and onto the grass. In desperation I squeezed her lips to allow the liquid to enter, but still there was no response. Crying out in frustration, I heaved her torso upright and hammered on her back. I pounded away until my hand hurt, but it was all to no avail. Ignoring my own discomfort I remained like that for some while before finally accepting the futility of it all. Then I gently eased Vicky's still warm body onto the ground and sat gazing at her with tears streaming down my face.

It was some time before I was able to regain a measure of self-control. With the return of logical thought came the awful realization of what I had heard. If somehow Vicky had managed to utter that name as she lay on the point of death, then it could only have been to warn me. For that one word to have been so important meant that Sarah Fetterman was now in extreme danger, from the man that I had come to regard as the devil incarnate!

Forcing myself to think rationally, I decided that if Vicky had, under extreme duress, told him of my relationship with Sarah, she must also have told him where to find her. Which meant that I would have to abandon both the rangers and the powder and ride pell mell for San Antonio de Béxar.

On the point of returning to my horse, a thought struck me. Had Speirs found the derringer? Intent on his perverted entertainment, he may not even have considered the possibility of her carrying a concealed weapon. After all, he had not even bothered to look for Kirby's revolver, a fact that had proven to be his undoing, and showed that he was not infallible. Gazing again on Vicky's agonized features, I felt strangely embarrassed at the thought of searching her body. There was a time when I would have welcomed the opportunity to delve under her dress, but this was not it. Partially averting my eyes, I hesitantly lifted the hem of her skirt, revealing a tantalizing glimpse of black stockings!

I supposed that they were only to be expected in her profession, but they had aroused my interest nonetheless. Pulling the material higher I exposed her creamy thighs and there, tucked in her stocking top was the small single shot weapon.

Pocketing the pistol, I stalked back to my horse and freed him from his hobble. I knew that I should return to the wagon and make my intentions plain, but there just wasn't the time. Every minute that I dallied could count against Sarah's survival. Speirs now had two mounts on which to alternate. He would be in San Antonio long before me. Mind made up, I clambered into the saddle. Within minutes I was over the first rise, and out of sight. For the first time in months I was truly alone.

CHAPTER TWELVE

For the remainder of that day I rode steadily west. My arm, although no longer supported by a sling, appeared to be on the mend. The wound had ceased to seep blood and the flesh seemed to be knitting together. Whatever torments that man had inflicted on me, there was no denying that he had quite probably saved the limb and possibly even my life. That did not sit well with everything else that had occurred and just served to highlight how nothing in life can be purely black or white.

With the lack of both company and distractions, I had plenty of time to brood over possible events in San Antonio. A resourceful man like Speirs would have little trouble locating Sarah, therefore I had to accept that by the time I arrived she would likely enough be his prisoner. He could not have foreseen that I would have found Vicky alive, if indeed she even had been.

Be that as it may, Speirs would know that Sarah was my Achilles heel and that I would make for her at my best speed. Which led me on to where he might take her. He would need shelter and by the very nature of his mission, would not want any interference. Yet he would most certainly wish to be found by me. Where in the environs of San Antonio de Béxar would he find a location to fulfil all these needs?

Barely had my fevered mind posed the question, when the answer presented itself. The Alamo Compound with its fortified church would be ideal. Empty and yet relatively close to the city, it would make a perfect location for him to hide away with his hostage. He could acquaint himself with the layout and await my arrival at leisure.

So certain was I that this scenario would take place, that I began to boil over with frustration. I was only able to contain my emotions due to the exertion required for riding. However, there is only so long that the mind can maintain a level of perpetual turmoil and by nightfall mine had burnt itself out. I was left with a core of ice cold rage, which was to stay with me for the remainder of that journey.

With the coming of darkness I decided against pushing on through the night. My body was still recovering and I would do little to enhance my cause by arriving worn out. Having rubbed down my horse, I dined on jerky and then resolved to allow myself a full night's sleep. Wrapping myself in my blanket, with a saddle for a pillow, I lay there gazing up at the night sky until suddenly it no longer existed.

On waking the following morning, I knew that that day would see me across the Guadalupe River and then San Antonio would finally be within reach. I was gratified to discover that I could lift the saddle into position far easier than at any time since my ordeal. And so, only a short time after rising, I was astride a horse and continuing west.

Around mid-afternoon I made out a clutch of trees up ahead and knew that I had reached the Guadalupe.

Heading straight for the sparkling liquid, I allowed the horse to drink before confidently traversing the benign watercourse. At that point a strange mood descended on me. I was happy to be within striking distance of my new home and yet I knew that the task before me could quite possibly claim my life. Dismounting briefly, I refilled my water canteen, stuffed my mouth with biscuits and within minutes was on my way again. Throughout that afternoon, whilst all the time brooding over the possible situation in San Antonio, I pressed my mount hard. By the time the light began to go, I had detected a change in the landscape ahead.

I spent that final night, quite conceivably my last one on earth, at the base of the Balcones Escarpment, knowing that on the morrow there was to be a reckoning. The escarpment itself was an area of hilly, wooded ground that led up to the far more inhospitable Edwards Plateau. San Antonio was situated some way up the escarpment and I fully expected to arrive there before nightfall the following day.

With this in mind, I meticulously checked and then double-checked my two weapons. Having used the last rays of light for this task, I again ate a cold supper of biscuits and beef jerky and then curled up in my blanket and tried to go to sleep. Yet myriad thoughts churned around in my head and I found it difficult to drift off. Graphically I explored various scenarios set in, and around, the Alamo Compound. Somehow I knew that I alone would have to deal with whatever situation awaited me.

I jerked upright bathed in sweat, convinced that I already was in the fortified church. The reality was actually far more mundane, as I took advantage of the morning light to view the emptiness around me. My heart was pounding, to the extent that it was some minutes before I had fully calmed down.

'God damn it all,' I cried out to a disinterested equine audience. 'One way or another it ends today!'

Having saddled the horse, stowed my belongings and attended to my toilet, I was off again at speed. In a fever of impatience to reach Sarah, I had to remind myself that such behaviour could get me killed. However it was the terrain, rather than any display of common sense, that effectively slowed me down, as I made my way up through the wooded hills of the escarpment.

As the morning progressed I knew that I was getting close, not so much because I was familiar with the ground, but more because I could sense it. And then the land began to level out and suddenly I knew where I was. The San Antonio River Valley beckoned and my horse could smell the water. Approaching from the east as I was, I would find the Alamo between the city and myself. If I had guessed Speirs's intentions correctly, he could already have been ensconced somewhere in that warren of buildings. It all depended on how much of a lead he had maintained.

My only option was to proceed carefully on my chosen path, which as a first step required me to discover the situation in the city. Accordingly I swung off to the south, thereby avoiding the Alamo Compound by a good margin. All that time the thoughts of what could be occurring there were eating away at me. Passing level with the south wall, I could just make out the remains of the breastwork, which had served to delay the onslaught of the Mexican Army some nine years before. At that range and with broken ground between, it was highly unlikely that anybody occupying the structure would have spotted me. Maintaining my pace for another half mile brought me up with San Antonio itself.

Reining in, it was with mixed emotions that I observed the city. My relief at finally reaching my destination was boundless, yet that was tempered by the desperate uncertainty of what I would find there. I prayed that Captain Hays and the remainder of his ranger company would be there, as that would make my task so much easier.

As I drew nearer, I could make out the individual buildings and even signs of activity on the dirt streets. The massive San Fernando Cathedral stood out amongst all the other adobe buildings. In front of this church was the Main Plaza, site of numerous saloons and fandango halls. It was to this area that I intended to go first. If an unusual looking stranger had recently arrived asking questions, he would surely have attracted attention and the best place to catch up on local gossip was a tavern.

My arrival at a steady pace from the south was unlikely to be noticed by Speirs, even if he was indeed lodged somewhere in the compound. It was only as I reached the first of the adobe buildings that I realized that I too was noteworthy for my appearance alone. Having endured God knows how many nights on the trail, numerous violent conflicts and only one hot bath, anyone downwind of me would have been unhappily aware of my presence. In addition, my jacket was torn to shreds, I was covered in dried blood and I now sported a luxurious but filthy beard.

Sure enough, as I arrived in the plaza, various idlers viewed me with interest. Ignoring them, I looked around to get my bearings. My destination was a small saloon next to the Béxar Exchange, an infamous fandango hall home to many ladies of the night. The proprietor of the saloon was a Joseph Wetsall, with whom I had become reasonably well acquainted during my time in San Antonio. I was convinced that he would have either seen or heard of Speirs's arrival. What I had not expected was his reaction to my own entrance.

The saloon was in no way comparable to the one that I had visited in Galveston, in either size or comfort, but it was an agreeable enough place to while away an evening. Having dismounted and tethered my horse, I walked stiffly inside and immediately spotted Wetsall wiping down the long counter that served as a bar. He was a slightly built man, of medium height, whom I had always found to be very affable.

'Good day, Joseph,' I called out. 'I am indeed happy to be back here.'

That worthy twisted round to look at me, his eyes narrowing as he struggled with my unaccustomed facial hair. Then, with a gasp, he fell back against the wall clutching his chest. 'Holy mother of God, this can't be!'

Both surprised and puzzled at this response, I advanced on him, hand outstretched in greeting. 'It is I, Thomas Collins. Pray forgive my repellent appearance, only I have been on the trail these many days past.'

'No,' he choked out by way of reply, his narrow face ashen. 'You were killed on the Colorado by those blamed savages!'

CHAPTER THIRTEEN

Hugo Speirs had yet again proved how devilishly clever he was. Having reached San Antonio the previous evening, he had made straight for the Main Plaza and announced himself as a travelling companion of mine. Conveniently discovering a saloon keeper that knew me, he had pronounced me dead at the hands of Comanches and then asked the whereabouts of a certain Sarah Fettermen, so that he could report my demise.

With a sinking heart I demanded of Wetsall, 'And you told him?'

'Why the hell not?' His response was offered defensively and with a deal of indignation. 'He had news of your death and he knew who to ask for.'

So that maniac had Sarah! So far things had gone as I had expected, which was absolutely no consolation at all.

'And there's something else as well,' continued Wetsall gloomily. 'He hired himself some bar trash. Said he needed men who would fight for pay, to help the rangers get your gunpowder back. They were queuing up when he flashed one of them fancy gold coins.'

Things were just getting worse. 'Where are Hays and his rangers?'

'Out tracking some Comanches, what raided the

Chambers' place. Been gone nigh on three days now.'

My head was aching. I desperately needed to work out what to do, but this saloon was not the place for that. Yet I did have another question. 'Was Speirs wounded?'

Wetsall nodded swiftly. 'Seemed to be favouring his left shoulder and like you was a mite splashed with blood. It all made sense, what with him tangling with the Comanche and all.' A look of exasperation came to his face, 'Thomas, *what's* going on?'

With a sigh, I told him of Speirs's real reason for coming to the city. The saloon keeper was visibly upset. Although a hard-nosed businessman, he was basically decent and seemed to harbour a liking for me. After hearing my story he was keen to make amends and immediately put the question, 'What can I do to help?'

There were two things that came directly to mind. 'I need Hays found and brought back here. There is gunpowder and it is destined for the rangers. Any riders that you can recruit will be paid, only not just yet. At this moment, thanks to Speirs, I am penniless.'

The other man smiled grimly as he replied, 'I'll see what I can do, anything else?'

'I need the shotgun that you keep under the counter. If that bastard's bought himself some help with my money, then I will need to even up the odds a little.'

The saloon keeper appeared distinctly uncomfortable as he considered my request. I knew that it was a lot to ask. That weapon was essential for controlling some of the wilder characters that frequented his establishment. So without giving him time to refuse, I added, 'For one night only. This time tomorrow it'll all be over, one way or another.'

'And if you get killed again,' he said, hefting the weapon under my nose, 'what happens to this beauty?'

Reaching out to take it in a firm grip, I said, 'Then it will be in the wrong hands and you'll need to look for a new method of crowd control!'

The single storey adobe building that was our home proved to be empty, yet displayed all the signs of a fierce struggle. It took all my self-control to stop myself from rushing blindly over to the compound. My only chance was to utilize the cover of darkness. Settling myself down next to the overturned bed, I checked over my expanding armoury, paying particular attention to my newest acquisition. Wetsall's shotgun appeared to be in good condition. It was well oiled and the caps were well seated. The barrel was far longer than I was used to, but it would suffice.

Finally the light began to ebb and I told myself that the time had come. Getting stiffly to my feet, I began stretching and twisting my body to loosen up, ready for the exertion ahead. Through the open door, I could hear the sounds of horses and men's voices. My heart leapt. Could it be the rangers returning from their pursuit? But no, it turned out to be some freighters gratefully reaching the city limits before nightfall. Swiftly appraising the light, I decided that I could now safely leave the building without being spotted from The Alamo. Consciously closing the heavy door behind me, I strode off to the Plaza.

A short time later I was back at the edge of the city, having obtained answers to three questions. Speirs had four men with him, the rangers had not returned and as far as Wetsall was concerned, he knew of nobody currently utilizing the Alamo Compound. It was generally accepted that Hays and his men used it as a powder store and so the citizenry kept well clear of it. I sincerely hoped that that was the case, as I would be treating every man in there as a deadly enemy.

The activity had served to keep me occupied until the darkness had become total. Although there was a sizable moon, it was obscured by heavy cloud, which I fervently hoped would remain overhead. Ensuring that any lamps behind me would not highlight my presence, I commenced walking steadily towards The Alamo. I knew that my present line of march would take me directly to the long West Wall, where there was a small sally port, through which I had entered the compound some weeks before to meet with Captain Hays. As it offered the easiest and therefore most obvious point of entry, I intended to keep well clear of it.

Instead, I began to veer off to my right, so as to come around the side of the south wall. It was here that I would find the remains of the breastwork, constructed to protect both the low wall and the barrack block immediately behind it. A ditch had been dug around it, which in the dark would create shadows, likely to assist a lone assailant. I thanked the Lord that, as a military man, I had been sufficiently interested in the old structure, to take the time to study it carefully in the months after I had arrived in Béxar County.

After walking strongly for a brief period, I was able to discern the outline of the old mission ahead of me. As planned, I was on course to arrive at the conjuncture of the south and west walls. For a short while longer I continued, but at a much-reduced speed, until I could clearly make out the walls before me. Then, taking care that nothing solid should collide with my weapons, I carefully dropped down to the ground, so that I laid completely flat.

Lying totally still, I watched and waited. Up against five men holding a hostage, I could count only on surprise as my ally. Although Speirs would doubtless be expecting me, he could not know when or from where I would approach. Which meant that he would have to spread his force very thinly to cover the main vantage points. Sooner or later one of his ill disciplined rabble would move, or clear his throat, or do something to give away his position.

I did not have long to wait. From atop the mound I heard a muffled cough and simultaneously saw a slight movement. Visualizing the breastwork as horseshoe shaped, I placed the individual at the closed end, furthest away from the compound. From there he would be able to see the whole of the south wall, as well as the surrounding countryside. Or at least he could have done had there been any light.

Silencing that man had to be my first objective. Tilting my body slightly, I retrieved my revolver and placed it on the ground next to Wetsall's shotgun. They were too cumbersome and would have to be recovered after the deed was done. Although I retained the derringer in my pocket, for this task I would be relying solely on my hunting knife. Without taking my eyes off the human silhouette, I got slowly to my feet and crept forward. If there should prove to be anyone else on the south wall, I was finished.

Silently I moved towards the ditch. Once there, I was confident that I would be able to find a way up into the strongpoint. When the Mexicans stormed the compound, they had used teams of fearsome soldiers known as pioneers to smash through the defences. The resultant damage had been left unrepaired, a fact that I was about to take advantage of. Creeping into the ditch, I now had to trust to luck, for if my prey should shift position I would be none the wiser.

Using a combination of sight and touch, I was able to move stealthily up the earthen bank until I reached the remains of the wooden fence. Thanks to the previous assault there were enough gaps in it to allow me access. Holding myself in place as best I could with my left arm, I drew my knife, all the time watching for the slightest movement within the fortification.

Then I saw him!

A stooped figure shuffled into view, yawned once, then turned and climbed up onto an empty gun platform facing east. I would not get any better chance than that. My entire body seemed to tingle with feverish anticipation.

Hardening my heart, I leapt through the gap in the fence and launched myself at the figure before me. Alerted by my footfalls he tried to turn, but his reaction time was woefully slow. Slamming into him with all my weight, I succeeded in crushing him against the wooden stakes. The wind was knocked out of him and along with it went any chance of resistance. Wrapping my left hand over his mouth, I brought my knife up to his throat and sliced in deep. Warm blood spurted over my chest, as a tremendous shudder of almost sexual intensity travelled through his frame. It continued for what seemed like an eternity before finally all movement ceased. My victim would have collapsed on the spot, had he not been trapped between the fence and myself. I was now irrevocably committed, and God help me if I'd killed in error!

To avoid even the slightest chance of generating noise, I supported the limp body until I was convinced that all life had departed. Then I gently lowered him to the ground, all the while aware of his blood, warm and sticky, on my hands and shirt. I was trembling slightly, as to kill a human being in that manner was both very intimate and very unpleasant.

Crouching down, I stared at the south wall and in particular the gate leading through it, for any sign that I might have been discovered. All I could hear was the faint sound of voices travelling on the still night air from San Antonio. Satisfied, I wiped my knife clean on the man's jacket, sheathed it and then searched him for weapons. Tucked in his belt, I discovered two single shot percussion pistols. The modest increase in firepower that they represented was not worth the additional weight, but I knew that they might prove useful as weapons of 'last resort'. Accordingly, I moved over to where I had entered the breastwork and placed them next to the fence. Then, easing through a gap, I slid back down into the ditch.

Having recovered my discarded firearms, I retraced my steps and had soon re-entered the defensive structure. Through the gate lay the disused barracks block, built against part of the south wall. It was my intention to pass through that and make for the fortified church.

'Usaph!'

The voice had emanated from the barracks and caused me to freeze like a statue. Desperately I forced myself to think clearly. If I didn't answer there were two possible outcomes. Either the speaker would investigate alone, in which case I could try my hand, or he would summon help and I would quite possibly have to flee.

'Usaph, you whore's son, answer me!'

That was all the prompting I needed. Keeping my voice low I growled out, 'Yo.'

That drew a swift and impatient response. 'Yo, he said. You playing with yourself or what?'

Again I tried to inject a certain huskiness to disguise my voice, as I gave the most minimal of responses. 'Huh?'

At the same time I laid down my shotgun, and again drew my knife. Silently I padded towards the left hand side of the gate. From the building I could hear muffled cursing, but the man's next remarks to Usaph were much louder, indicating that the speaker had moved closer. 'English'll have your cojones if you fall asleep!'

He obviously intended investigating Usaph's condition, so I pressed my shoulder against the wall and gripped my knife at waist height. The measured steps of someone moving carefully in the dark were audible in the gate-house. Even though the night was cool, I could feel beads of sweat forming on my forehead as the tension built up inside of me again.

A large shape appeared at the entrance and then he was upon me. Lunging forward, I was aware of two things. The man was huge and he carried a revolver in his right hand. Using my left shoulder to barge his weapon aside, I plunged my blade into his vast gut. The overwhelming shock caused his right forefinger to contract and with a roar his revolver discharged close to my head. The blast from the muzzle was stupefying, yet I was also aware of various burning sensations on my face and neck.

As pain engulfed my opponent he bellowed like a wounded bear, but kept on coming. In danger of being bowled over by such a man mountain, I gave my knife a vicious twist before pulling it free. Both of us had abruptly lost our night vision, with the effect that we were left struggling in a fog. My left arm was paining me abominably from such rough usage and I knew that my only chance of stopping the behemoth was to keep stabbing. So, like a berserker, I plunged the blade into his belly again and again. His warm blood spurted out over my hand and arm, but still he stayed on his feet. I couldn't comprehend how any man could absorb such hideous injuries. Then, with an almost animal like keening sound, he dropped to his knees.

To the accompaniment of a ghastly sucking sound, I withdrew my knife for the last time and staggered back.

Like a tree that wouldn't fall, the creature before me remained on his knees, swaying slightly as though in the face of a breeze. My vision was beginning to return, but I was left with a persistent ringing in my left ear.

The revolver's deafening report had undoubtedly destroyed my advantage of surprise and confirmation of this fact was not long in coming. From well beyond the barracks block came the sound of confused shouting, all of it in recognizable Texan accents. The individual that I was seeking abruptly curtailed all this. Speirs's cultured, yet noticeably strident tones cried out, 'Be silent, damn your eyes! If you expect a penny piece for this night's work, you will close on me now.'

Silence did indeed return to the compound, but one thing had irrevocably altered. I now knew for certain that any more killing that took place that night was justified, and also that the 'English' referred to earlier would not see another sunrise.

CHAPTER FOURTEEN

Whatever manoeuvres Speirs was contemplating, I knew that I was far too vulnerable out in the open. Momentarily I wondered whether the shot had aroused any interest in the city, but soon concluded that an occasional gunshot would not be unusual in a frontier settlement. Guardedly viewing the huge man still on his knees before me, I noticed that the revolver had slipped from his hand. The front of his linen shirt had almost disintegrated, with what was left apparently stained black under the night sky. From the short gasps of breath that he was taking, I realized that he was only just clinging to life. Impatient to be off and with absolutely no sympathy for his suffering, I kicked him hard in the chest with my right foot. Like a great oak crashing to earth, he fell back and to the side, coming to rest on the exact spot where I had first entered the breastwork. Swiftly I scooped up his Colt revolver, followed by my shotgun. Then, without any hesitation, I swept into the gatehouse, only to turn a sharp right through another door into the barrack block itself.

As my eyes adjusted to the different level of gloom, I inspected my new surroundings. There was one doorway, with a battered wooden door hanging open. Two windows faced onto the compound. These both possessed metal fittings on either side, but the shutters belonging to them had long since been removed. Surprisingly the interior held a well-worn selection of chairs, tables and even a few wooden cot frames.

Knowing that it would be suicide to venture out into the open compound without having any idea where my opponents were, I quickly dragged a table over to the doorway. Quietly pushing the door closed, I then pitched the table on its side and wedged it tight. As I stepped back into the room the unmistakable tones of Hugo Speirs boomed out. 'Good evening, Major Collins. Because of course it can only be you. How else could I explain the loss of two new recruits to my cause?'

As he paused for breath, I moved over to the first window. I had no intention of looking out, but I hoped to be better able to gauge where his voice was coming from.

'Nothing to say, Thomas? What a shame. I was so hoping to renew our acquaintance. There are few people of culture in this godforsaken land.'

The bastard was definitely located somewhere off to my right, very probably in the church, as I had considered earlier. But how was I to get to him?

'If you won't talk to me, perhaps this delightful young lady will loosen your tongue.'

There followed a short period of silence, followed by a sudden scream of pain. Rage welled up inside me, but before I had chance to react Sarah's voice called out. 'Keep clear, Thomas, you hear? He means to have you when—'

Her voice abruptly ceased, to be followed swiftly by that of Speirs. 'You will throw down your weapons, all of them and walk out into the open. Otherwise this young lady will no longer be delightful, or even for that matter alive. Do I make myself clear?'

The bantering tone had gone, replaced by one of deadly intent. I longed to throw myself on him like a rabid dog, but such thoughts would not serve. I had to retain a clear head. The danger in my replying was obvious, but I could not ignore such a threat. So, keeping clear of the windows, I launched into a spirited response. 'My weapons are the only things keeping us both alive, as you well know. If you kill her you will never take me back. The rangers already know of your murderous activities and are on their way here as we speak. Your only chance is to leave now and try to make for the coast, alone! If you do that, you have my word that I'll not hinder you.'

Such a lie tripped easily off my tongue, but I nearly paid for it with my life. My impassioned defiance had made me careless. Only as I finished speaking did I remember that Speirs was not alone. A split second after I hit the dirt floor, a volley of shots smashed into the window surround and the stonework behind me. As the twin detonations rang out in the night, I felt shards of masonry tumble on to me.

Tightly grasping my borrowed shotgun, I rolled to my feet and scrambled for the back of the room. From there I could see out, but would be invisible to anyone beyond the windows. I realized immediately where the assassin was concealed. Some twenty-five yards into the compound was a gun emplacement directly facing the gatehouse through which I had entered. Somewhere behind that earthen mound he was lurking, very probably recharging his weapon. A frontal assault was out of the question, especially as there was at least one other man out there in the dark. To return through the gatehouse and then out beyond the walls made no sense. Which left me with the roof!

Placing a table next to the wall, I clambered up to test

its resistance. As I could already touch the ceiling from the ground, the additional height enabled me to put my back to it. Immediately there was a satisfying crack, as the worn timber slats gave way. Only the roofs destined to support cannon had been reinforced by the Alamo's defenders. Trusting to luck that no one would approach the windows, I turned all my efforts onto tearing a hole wide enough to climb through. In a matter of minutes I had forced a gap. By standing upright on the table, I could see that a low wall of sufficient height to conceal me, surrounded the roof.

Thinking fast, I returned to the floor, grabbed a chair and then thrust that up through the opening. Following that with the shotgun, I then regained the table and heaved myself up onto the roof. Whatever happened now, I was safe from an immediate assault. Crawling over to the front of the building, I risked a quick look. Through the gloom and with the benefit of height, I could see a figure moving about behind the emplacement. The lack of any response to his ambuscade was obviously working on his nerves. With his weapon reloaded, he was undoubtedly itching to move.

If I was to take advantage of my situation I had to act fast. Off to my right stood another one-storey building that had served as a kitchen. Moving back from the edge, I got to my knees, took hold of the chair and hurled it with all my strength. As planned, it flew along a forty-five degree angle and crashed into the roof of that structure. My assailant's response was instantaneous. The shotgun crashed out once and the kitchen roofline received a hail of missiles.

Having sat down on the low wall, I then dropped just over six feet, rolled on my right shoulder and raced off down my left flank at another forty-five degree angle. Drawing parallel with the gun emplacement, I twisted sharply to the right, levelled my own shotgun and squeezed the trigger. With a roar, the first barrel discharged. Immediately I dashed a few paces to my left and dropped to the ground, so that I was now behind the emplacement. From there another shotgun blast sounded and from the position of the powder flash, it was aimed directly at the spot that I had just vacated. So now I knew exactly where he was!

My own weapon recoiled brutally against my shoulder, as I detonated the second charge. I received an intoxicating whiff of sulphur as the powder smoke drifted over me, and from a few short yards away a high-pitched scream rent the night air. I was given no time to bask in my success as, again from off to my left, a revolver fired. The ball slammed into the ground close to my face, blasting bits of earth into my hair. My position was untenable, as the gunman appeared to know my location exactly. Abandoning Wetsall's weapon, I jumped up and sprinted over to the gun emplacement and the continued screaming of its occupant.

It was swiftly apparent why that man was in such distress. He had taken the bulk of my discharge in his face and although still alive, was just a tormented wreck. Quite obviously blind, he was pawing at his face, desperately trying to obtain some relief. My first inclination was to end his suffering, but the tenuousness of my own situation forced me to harden my heart. Somewhere over near the church lurked the last of the captain's henchmen and the blubbering ruin next to me provided me with a way to destroy him.

There was another detonation over by the church and a ball ploughed into the earth wall next to me. The man concealed there either assumed that his companion was dead, or simply didn't care. Taking hold of the wounded man's jacket, I heaved him to his feet. Out of his mind with pain he did not resist, but just continued with his sobbing and whining. I swiftly realized that I could not both support and manoeuvre him with one hand. Both belt guns would have to remain tucked in there, whilst I manhandled my human shield. I had possibly nine chambers available to me, provided the big man's revolver had been fully loaded when I attacked him.

Positioning myself directly behind my prisoner, I pressed my knee into the small of his back to propel him forward. Knowing only suffering and oblivious to my intention, he stumbled forward. And all the time, in the recesses of my mind, was the nagging worry over the location of Hugo Speirs.

It became apparent that whomever we were approaching at least had his wits about him, as an angry voice boomed out across the compound. 'For God's sake, Jeb, get down. I can't get a shot at him!'

If this were going to work I would have to force the pace. Ignoring Jeb's cries for aid, I kept my hands under his armpits and together we lurched towards the church. Another shot rang out, but this time much closer. The ball hit somewhere near our feet. I knew that it would be the only warning shot. The deadly nature of our progress seemed to have filtered through to Jeb, as he began to struggle in my grip.

'Hold still,' I snarled, as I pressed remorselessly onward. Then the inevitable happened. The next report was so loud that I felt I could reach out and touch my opponent. The ball penetrated Jeb's chest at close range, the impact almost knocking us both down. The effect on him was immediate, as all strength left his legs.

Allowing his dead weight to fall away from me, I drew and cocked both revolvers. The two weapons bucked in my hands and the resultant flashes provided brief but limited illumination. It was sufficient to highlight a human form, as it ducked down behind the low wall that separated the church from the rest of the compound.

Always fire and move!

I ran for the cover of the kitchen, the roof of which I had earlier hurled a chair at. This backed onto the same low wall and also joined up with the barrack block where I had taken refuge. With both revolvers again fully cocked, I burst into the darkened room and crouched down behind the only window. Drawing in deep drafts of air, I tried to steady myself. Since my murderous attack on Usaph, I had been in almost perpetual motion. I was hot and sweaty and my left arm ached abominably.

Gradually my breathing returned to normal and I became aware that an almost eerie silence had settled over the compound. Such a situation worked on the nerves, and was far harder to cope with than the heat of battle.

'Hello, Thomas!'

Speirs's voice came from directly behind me, but some distance back into the room. It came as a complete surprise and left me frozen with shock.

'You never fail to entertain me with your resourcefulness. I will be almost sad to hand you over to the authorities.' His tone was one of light-hearted banter, but I knew that it had to be backed up by deadly force. As if to confirm my thoughts and right on cue, I heard the distinctive sound of a hammer being retracted.

'I have my Pepperbox in the other hand, but as you doubtless know that does not require cocking. I could kill you now, but that would only complicate things. So if you resist I shall merely provide you with a disabling and excruciatingly painful wound.' He said this with such confidence that he could almost have been bored with the proceedings. 'Now, I will thank you to place your two revolvers on the ground. Do not stand up or turn around.'

As I complied with his command, my mind was a seething cauldron. He could not know of Vicky's derringer in my pocket, yet I had no opportunity to reach for it. Nothing would induce me to be his prisoner again, yet I had Sarah's survival to consider.

'Where is Sarah? What have you done with her?'

His reply was instantaneous, yet delivered in that strange, almost carefree manner of his. 'Oh, she's hanging around somewhere. If you follow my instructions to the letter I might allow you to see her.'

An icy tremor went through my body at the implications of that reply, but I determined to remain strong. Feigning concern I asked, 'And how is your shoulder, Hugo? Does it pain you a lot?'

'I am indebted to your ranger friend for that. I intend to repay him in full at my convenience.' A noticeably harsher edge had crept into his voice. I wondered whether he was actually capable of holding two weapons.

His next instruction showed that there was nothing amiss with his wits. 'For now though, I require you to drop your knife on the ground and then stand up.'

This was the moment. If I failed to act, I would consign Sarah and myself to oblivion. With an exaggerated sigh, I tossed my knife away to one side and slowly raised myself up out of the crouching position. Before reaching my full height I fell forward and simply rolled out of the window. The fact that I survived the manoeuvre was proof enough that I had caught him off guard.

As I scrabbled away to the side, a shot crashed out from the interior of the building and I knew that in such an enclosed space Speirs would probably be deaf for some time to come. Getting properly to my feet, I ran for my life towards the gatehouse.

Now sounding anything but light-hearted, Speirs yelled out to his one remaining accomplice. 'Get after him, you oaf, he's making for the gatehouse. He's unarmed!'

That last comment probably saved my life. As I reached the entrance, another shot rang out, but the weapon was fired on the move and the ball merely smacked into masonry.

Charging into the gatehouse, I looked to neither left nor right, but continued on to the breastwork beyond. I left the building like a cork from a bottle and then angled over to my right. Twisting sharply, I allowed my back to slam into the wooden fence, this being the simplest way to halt my headlong dash. Ignoring the pain that that collision created, I reached down and grabbed my two weapons of 'last resort'. Pounding footsteps sounded in the gatehouse, as I somewhat clumsily cocked both long barrelled pistols at once. Without taking any precautions whatsoever, my pursuer charged out of the building at a dead run.

I will never forget the expression of sheer horror on his face, as he caught sight of the muzzles levelled at his torso. Both pistols crashed out in the night, their flashes highlighting the fate of my enemy. The impetus of the two heavy balls was sufficient to stop him in his tracks. Coughing blood, he slewed sideways and by a fitting quirk of fate, collapsed on top of the bear-like individual that I had dispatched earlier.

Bending over my latest victim, I dragged him onto his back. He was in possession of two Paterson Colt revolvers. One was in his belt, whilst the other was still gripped in his right hand. Taking hold of them both, I balanced them in my hands and drew the expected result. The belted weapon had expended five shots and was therefore empty; whilst on closer inspection the other appeared to be fully charged. Therefore, along with the 'stocking pistol', I now had six shots available to me. That would have to do. Discarding the empty weapon, I squeezed through a gap in the fence and slid down the east wall of the defensive breastwork. I had now dispatched all of Speirs's 'bar trash', and no power on earth was going to prevent me finding my beloved Sarah Fetterman.

CHAPTER FIFTEEN

Between the corner of the south wall and the church, lay a defensive structure known as the Palisade Wall. This had been constructed after the original compound, to link up the two walls and prevent anyone approaching the church, other than through the compound itself. A ditch ran along the full length of it. It was in this that I now scurried, like a rat through a run. I knew with an obsessive certainty that Sarah was somewhere in the church. Apart from it being the strongest defensive site, its appearance and history would undoubtedly appeal to Speirs's sense of theatre.

But if I was aware of that, so too would he. He seemed to possess an uncanny ability to second-guess my moves. Yet he was wounded and he did make mistakes. Consideration of his shoulder wound gave me the germ of an idea. Like my own injury it would hamper him from climbing, but by enduring the pain such a tactic had proved successful for me. Individual rooms in the church possessed roofs, yet that main hall of worship did not. If I could somehow get atop one of them, I would have a clear field of fire across what I knew as the nave.

In the time taken to ponder all of this, I had reached the south wall of the church. Its height and solidity was intimidating, but by keeping close to its contours I hoped to avoid being seen. Coming round to the east wall, I remembered that a gun emplacement had been constructed behind it, but again I had no way of scaling it. My one chance lay where the north wall of the church joined the low east wall of the compound. Here was the fortified church's only weakness and I intended to exploit it to the full.

I soon found myself standing at the juncture of the right angle where the two structures met. The compound wall was just over six feet high and I knew that behind it I would find a firing step running the full length of it. For well over a minute I just stood on the spot and listened. The silence was total. Placing my latest acquisition securely in my belt, I reached up and seized the top of the wall with my right hand.

Gritting my teeth, I raised my left arm up to join the other and gave a mighty heave. The effort provided enough momentum to allow me to swing a leg up onto the wall, but I very nearly blacked out. The pain was quite sufficient to make Heaven weep. Had Speirs been in the vicinity he would have caught me like a floundering fish. Lying flat on the wall, I could taste bile in my mouth. Blinking rapidly to clear my vision, I looked anxiously around. Mercifully all was quiet. Drawing in a deep breath to steady myself, I got carefully to my feet and viewed the next obstacle. Another climb of similar height awaited me, putting me atop a parapet similar to the one that I had dropped from earlier.

Anticipation of the discomfort to follow would only make it worse, so I simply threw myself at the structure and dragged my weary, pain wracked body over. I almost cried out in my torment, only managing to avoid it by keeping a vision of Sarah in my head.

Stifling a sob, I hauled myself off the parapet and down

onto another roof. It felt sound enough and displayed no sign of strain at supporting my weight. The next part would be deuced awkward. To look down into the church would involve the risk of discovery. Then I heard a low moan.

Crawling forward, I reached the edge and peered over. What I saw will remain etched in my mind for all time. I barely resisted the urge to bellow out my rage and indignation. Speirs's disconcertingly flippant remark had had a basis in truth. Sarah was quite literally 'hanging around'!

Ducking back behind the low wall, I tried to make sense of what I had just seen. That man had a sickness upon him for which there was only one cure.

Near the east wall of the church there remained an assortment of timber supports used to reinforce the gun platform. The captain had had two of these nailed together to form a crucifix. Sarah's slim form, clad only in a nightgown, had been tied to it, so that she bore an unnervingly close resemblance to Christ on the Cross. In an uncharacteristic gesture of compassion, the madman had restricted himself to the use of rawhide rather than nails.

Taking advantage of the moonlight, I risked another rapid scrutiny. It was obvious that the bonds were sufficiently tight to restrict her circulation, but what really concerned me was the cord around her neck. In addition, a rag of some sort was tied across her mouth, effectively stifling any cries for assistance and no doubt further impeding her breathing. The thought that Vicky's fate could be repeated was just too much to bear.

And then she looked up!

The light of the silvery orb permitted our eyes to meet and the sheer terror that she felt transmitted itself to me. She was imploring me to save her in the only way that she could.

An overwhelming sense of guilt hit me, as I knew only

too well that her suffering was purely due to her involvement with me. Then her eyes dropped with such rapidity
that only one explanation was possible. Speirs had to be
nearby.

Dipping back behind the wall, I steadily and deliberately
counted to sixty, before raising myself up again. Nothing
had changed. Then her eyes flitted back up to mine and I
carefully mouthed one word: '*Where?*'

She still had her wits about her and flashed a glance to
her left, to where a ramp led up to the gun platform. So
that was his location. Utilizing his innate cunning, Speirs
had positioned himself in the shadows somewhere under
the gun emplacement, enabling him to see anyone
approaching Sarah. By a combination of good judgement
and luck, I had avoided his field of vision.

The only way to flush the bastard out was to open fire on
him, but whilst the angle of our relative positions pre-
vented him seeing me, it also hindered such action. Then
I recalled the derringer. Removing it from my pocket I
tested its balance. Dropping it upside down at the correct
angle onto hard ground, so that the hammer struck first,
would hopefully cause the percussion cap to detonate. By
the grace of God, part of the nave had been stone flagged,
so providing the perfect surface.

Placing the Colt inside my jacket so as to muffle the
noise, I cocked the hammer and then placed it on the roof
before me. Taking the derringer in both hands, I leaned
very slightly over the wall so as to line it up with the ramp.
Then I simply let go of the diminutive pistol.

Almost instantaneously a loud report echoed through
the church, followed by the sound of an impact under the
gun platform. With a strident oath, Captain Hugo Speirs
leapt out into full view, desperately searching for his
assailant. In his right hand he held a Paterson Colt, whilst

his left arm was shrouded in a sling. Swiftly picking up my revolver, I took careful aim at his torso and squeezed the trigger. Emitting a loud bang, the weapon bucked satisfyingly in my hand.

The .36 calibre lead ball smashed into the officer's right shoulder, throwing him back into one of the timber supports. The captured revolver had obviously pulled to the left slightly, as I had intended to catch him dead centre. Speirs stood there with a stunned expression on his face, gazing down at the blood soaking into his jacket. A feeling of pure joy surged through me, as I realized that I had finally overcome my lethal adversary. Rising up on my knees so as to be in full view, I kept my weapon trained on him and shouted down, 'Throw the gun away, or I will surely finish you!'

Even as I uttered those words, I knew that I really should have just discharged another chamber and ended his life, but something held me back. The same misplaced sense of decency that I had exhibited with Sergeant Flaxton perhaps.

At first he showed no sign of having heard me, but then painfully slowly he raised his head and settled his eyes on mine. For long seconds he just stared at me, as though weighing up his options. Then, with a resigned sigh, he gently lowered the hammer to half cock and tossed the revolver off into the shadows.

'Now the Pepperbox!'

Speirs's only response was to allow his finely honed features to register a slight smile, and for an instant I thought that he just might resist. But no, discretion took the place of valour and he unhurriedly pulled the vicious looking weapon from the folds of his sling.

'Place it carefully on the floor,' I commanded.

For all his apparent calm he was obviously in great pain,

for the effort required to bend down elicited a tremendous groan from him.

'Now the knife,' I continued relentlessly. 'Throw it over towards Sarah.'

I would need that, having surrendered mine a short time before.

Without a word, he drew it from the sheath in his right boot and did as I commanded. The blade clattered against the flagstone as it came to rest near her feet. Motioning with my gun barrel towards the north wall I said, 'Now move over there and sit down.'

I expected some form of defiance, but again he obeyed without comment. Pushing himself away from the support, he staggered over to the wall. Blood continued to soak into his clothes and his darkly handsome face had turned ashen. As he collapsed to the floor, a cry of pain escaped his thin lips, but too much had passed between us for me to feel even the slightest compassion.

Placing my revolver in my belt, I swung over the parapet and dropped into the nave of the church. I hit the stone flags with my knees bent and then rolled onto my right shoulder. Crying out as a sharp pain shot through my ankles, I nevertheless twisted around rapidly to view my recumbent opponent. Such was the power of his personality; I still could not fully accept that I had vanquished him.

He lay with his back to the wall, apparently posing no threat. Getting gingerly to my feet, I limped over to where Sarah hung so pathetically from the cross. Taking up Speirs's knife, I stepped up to face her and again our eyes met. Smiling through a veil of tears, I carefully sliced the cord from around her neck and then removed the gag from her mouth. The skin around her lips was cracked and sore. I wanted to smother her in kisses, but knew that would have to wait. I then sliced through the cords that restrained her legs. As I did so, a tremendous shudder went through her lightly clad body. Next I cut away the rawhide that bound her arms so that, suddenly unsupported, she fell forward onto my right shoulder.

'Oh Thomas, I knew you'd come for me.' So saying she clung to me with the strength of ten, as her whole body began to tremble with reaction.

'What a touching little scene,' commented Speirs dryly from off to my left.

An icy chill swept up my back. Even though Sarah clung bodily to me I swivelled, reached down for my revolver and pointed it directly at him. He had uttered those same words an instant before destroying Kirkham Shockley! His right hand, on the point of entering the folds of the sling, froze as he observed my unexpectedly swift reaction.

Without taking my eyes from him, I gently but firmly detached myself from Sarah and allowed her to slip to the ground. The cold fury that had enveloped me throughout my final journey to San Antonio returned, as I strode over to the north wall.

'Remove the sling,' I bellowed. 'Now!'

For the first time, an air of uncertainty clouded his features. With the gaping muzzle of my revolver pointing directly at his head, he had little option other than to comply. Slowly, and showing genuine discomfort, he removed the material and placed it on the floor with a resounding thump.

As the toe of my boot slipped into it, the cloth shifted to reveal yet another revolver. Belatedly, I realized that it was only his arrogant overconfidence that had saved me, or rather us!

The knowledge that my earlier inability to end his life had again put Sarah's in jeopardy sent me into a paroxysm of rage. I lashed out with unrestrained ferocity. The barrel of my weapon smashed into the side of his head, sending him sideways onto the stone floor. As he lay there unresisting, I kicked him repeatedly. Finally, I stepped back and again levelled my piece.

Battered and bruised he may have been, but his wits remained as sharp as ever.

'You haven't got the guts to kill me in cold blood,' he snarled, fixing his cool eyes on mine. 'I'm a British officer on active duty, and you're supposedly my superior, at least in rank.'

Even in his position he could not resist baiting me, but he had succeeded in one respect. He was still alive. As though sensing my indecision, he kept pushing. 'And what about your arm? If I had not extracted that arrowhead, greenrod would have set in and you'd be dead. *That low bred bitch would never have seen you again.*'

Even as he said that he acknowledged his mistake. Ignoring the pain, I reached forward with that very arm, grabbed a handful of greasy black hair and yanked him to his feet. As he swayed unsteadily before me, I prodded him viciously in the belly with my gun muzzle.

'*Outside,*' I barked.

Through the double doors we plodded and onto the low wall that I had earlier considered vaulting. Finally we reached the main compound.

Speirs could not contain himself any longer. 'Where the devil are you taking me?'

Shoving him forward, I gestured towards the Alamo's well. 'You're going for a little swim,' I replied venomously.

Hugo Speirs's eyes widened in horror as he took in the full implication of my statement, but he still made one last attempt. 'Sergeant Flaxton told me how you had him under your knife, yet you just couldn't finish him!'

Backing him up against the lip of the stone well, I met

his gaze and favoured him with a mirthless smile. 'Where is he now then?'

With that, I hammered the barrel of the Colt against his cheekbone and then shoved hard against his chest. Stunned by the unexpected blow, he could not resist the sudden pressure. Toppling backwards, his legs swiftly disappeared from view as he plummeted down the shaft. He was not even able to cry out before hitting the water and then there was only silence. Falling head first down a narrow bore with injuries such as his, meant that death by drowning was inevitable. Belatedly, I also realized that recovering my gold sovereigns was going to require a lot of effort!

Footfalls sounded behind me. 'What have you done, Thomas?'

Turning, I found Sarah regarding me with a mixture of confusion and relief. Her nightgown was badly torn and she was showing a deal more leg than was proper in those parts.

'What I've been trying to do for weeks. What *Vicky* would have wanted.'

'Vicky?'

On the point of answering, I was abruptly halted by a dramatic entrance. Prefaced by the pounding of many hoofs, a column of riders swept into the compound. Catching sight of us near the well they spread out and advanced menacingly across the moonlit ground. Making no attempt to raise my revolver, I turned to face them as they formed up around us in a semi-circle.

One rider moved slightly to the fore of the others, indicating that he was the acknowledged leader. Slim and slightly built, he made no attempt to reach for a weapon. Instead he settled his piercing eyes on mine and in a strangely high voice said, 'Good evening, Major Collins. I trust I find you well and in possession of *our* gunpowder!'

With somewhat mixed feelings, I greeted the return of Captain John Coffee Hays.

CHAPTER SIXTEEN

Along with ushering in a new day, the sunrise brought with it an amazing spectacle. Jack Hays, Sarah Fetterman and a somewhat battered Thomas Collins rode at the head of a column of fourteen heavily armed Texas Rangers. We were on our way down the escarpment to, God willing, meet with and assist Kirby and his much-reduced party. Sarah, in the face of much protest and even some mild threats, had insisted on accompanying the force.

'You done left me for the last time, Thomas Collins. You might think you're as fast as shit from a goose, but look at the state of you.'

The remainder of the previous night had been spent explaining to the Ranger Captain why so much Texan blood had been spilt in the Alamo Compound, followed by a few hours' sleep snatched before the dawn. Though we had so much to talk about, Sarah and I had agreed to hold off for another time. For her body to be curled up next to mine on our bed was quite sufficient for me. It was the first time that I had felt truly safe for weeks.

The ride out from San Antonio afforded the time for me to explain the circumstances surrounding the purchase and transportation of the precious gunpowder. Hays listened intently. It was not until I had finished off with talk of my arrival in San Antonio that he finally spoke. Glancing over at Sarah before fixing his gaze firmly on me he said, 'Although neither of you would agree with me, I am compelled to say that this man Speirs did you a service by carrying Sarah off.'

I made to protest, but he cut me off. 'Four citizens of San Antonio were brutally slain and a visiting British national heaved down a well by you, sir! Doubtless they needed killing, but that would have been hard to justify on your word alone, had it not been for the disgraceful kidnapping of this lady. Such action changed everything, as the capture of women and children by the Comanches is an all too familiar occurrence out here. Such behaviour will not be tolerated.' Then his expression softened. 'By the by, would you happen to know what the date was yesterday?'

I was totally flummoxed. Not only had I no idea of the date, I couldn't for the life of me understand the relevance of his question. A pleading glance at Sarah elicited no help, so my answer was merely an elaborate shrug of the shoulders.

Hays laughed again, as though at a private joke, before enlightening us both. 'February 23rd, 1845. Nine years to the day since the siege of the Alamo began. In your own way you managed to commemorate it quite well.'

As the day progressed, storm clouds began to build and it appeared as though our run of unseasonably dry weather was coming to a close. I had made it my business to accompany the relief column for two reasons. I wished to be on hand personally when Captain Hays appropriated the first wagonload of powder and I also keenly desired to greet

Sergeant Kirby, with whom I had shared so much.

Hays had tactfully left Sarah and I alone, so that we were able to ride together companionably without being over-heard. It was me who first raised the subject of her cousin, albeit with some trepidation.

'Why didn't you tell me after your husband was killed that you had Vicky for a cousin? I could perhaps have found her for you last year and avoided this tragedy.'

Sarah favoured me with a sad smile. 'Because she was a strumpet! She paid her way by selling her body and that ain't nothing to be proud of. I'm right sorry she's dead, but what's done is done.' Then she settled her piercing green eyes on mine as she remarked, 'I hope she didn't offer you anything on account, because *she* ain't here to settle with, only you.'

My guts were bubbling like hot tar, but I managed to maintain a calm exterior as I answered that. 'What kind of man do you take me for? She was your cousin, for God's sake.'

She smiled, but couldn't resist one last salvo. 'That's good, because if I thought anything had passed betwixt you two, I'd be the meanest bitch that ever bawled for beads!'

That was the last reference she made of cousin Vicky, but the thought of the two of them under one roof turned my bowels to mush.

The outrider reined in before his captain, a broad smile on his face. 'It's them all right, Jack. One wagon and four men, down near the base of the escarpment.'

Hays's thin face lit up with sheer joy and as the news passed down the column, shouting and cheering broke out. Rain began to patter down, but I knew that no amount of it could dampen our spirits. Increasing his pace, the captain led us down through the trees, until sure enough we were all able to see the small party moving towards us.

With a surge of emotion, I identified Travis, Davey and Ben sitting together on the bench seat, waving and shouting themselves hoarse. Kirby, astride his mount, was altogether more restrained. As we drew closer, I was shocked to discover that they resembled street beggars, with their unkempt beards and torn, filthy clothing. That feeling was compounded, when it came to me that I too was in the same state.

Making straight for Kirby, I reined in before him. Reaching out, I accepted his proffered hand. Seemingly oblivious to the joyous mayhem around us, we remained like that for a long moment. It was Kirby who first broke the reflective silence between us.

'Reckon I'm right glad to see you all,' he offered laconically. Thoughtfully massaging his disfigured neck he continued, 'And what of that festering cockchafer Speirs?'

'He's dead!'

'Figured he might be. He die hard?'

'Very!'

'Any others along with him?'

'Four.'

'You counted, huh?'

'It makes sense in my profession.'

'And what might that be, Thomas?'

I thought about that for some time before answering. 'Soldier of fortune,' I finally replied with a broad grin.